S0-AFA-295

BOOKS BY ORIANA FALLACI

The Useless Sex
Penelope at War
Egotists: Sixteen Surprising Interviews
If the Sun Dies
Nothing, and So Be It
Interview with History
Letter to a Child Never Born

ORIANA FALLACI

Letter to a Child Never Born

TRANSLATED BY JOHN SHEPLEY

SIMON AND SCHUSTER · NEW YORK

PUBLISHED BY SIMON AND SCHUSTER

A DIVISION OF GULF & WESTERN CORPORATION
SIMON & SCHUSTER BUILDING
ROCKEFELLER CENTER
1230 AVENUE OF THE AMERICAS
NEW YORK, NEW YORK 10020

DESIGNED BY EVE METZ
MANUFACTURED IN THE UNITED STATES OF AMERICA

3 4 5 6 7 8 9 10

LIBRARY OF CONGRESS CATALOGING IN PUBLICATION DATA
FALLACI, ORIANA.
LETTER TO A CHILD NEVER BORN.
TRANSLATION OF LETTERA A UN BAMBINO MAI NATO.
I. TITLE.
PZ4.F192LE [PQ4866.A4] 858'.9'14 76–45205
ISBN 0–671–22374–7

To those who do not fear doubt—
To those who wonder why
without growing tired and at the cost
of suffering and dying—
To those who pose themselves the dilemma
of giving life or denying it—
this book is dedicated
by a woman
for all women.

Letter to a Child Never Born

LAST NIGHT I KNEW you existed: a drop of life escaped from nothingness. I was lying, my eyes wide open in the darkness, and all at once I was certain you were there. You existed. It was as if a bullet had struck me. My heart stopped. And when it began to pound again, in gun bursts of wonder, I had the feeling I had been flung into a well so deep that everything was unsure and terrifying. Now I am locked in fear that soaks my face, my hair, my thoughts. I am lost in it. It is not fear of others. I don't care about others. It's not fear of God. I don't believe in God. It's not fear of pain. I have no fear of pain. It is fear of you, of the circumstance that has wrenched you out of nothingness to attach yourself to my body. I was never eager to welcome you, even though I've known for some time that you might exist someday. In that sense I have long awaited you. But still I've always asked myself the terrible question: What if you don't want to be born? What if some day you were to cry out to reproach me: "Who asked you to bring me into the world, why did you bring me into it, why?" Life is such an effort, Child. It's a war that is renewed each day, and its moments of joy are brief parentheses for which you pay a cruel price. How can I know that it wouldn't be better to throw you away? How can I tell that you wouldn't rather be returned to the silence? You cannot speak to me; your drop of life is only a cluster of cells that has scarcely begun. Perhaps it's not even life, only the mere possibility of life. I wish that you could help me with even a nod, a slight sign. My mother claims that I gave her such a sign, and that was the reason she brought me into the world.

You see, my mother didn't want me. I was begun in a moment of other people's carelessness. And hoping I wouldn't be born, she dissolved some medicine in a glass of water each night. Then, weeping, she drank it. She drank it faithfully until the night I moved inside her belly and gave her a kick to tell her not to throw me away. She was lifting the glass to her lips when I signaled. She turned it upside down immediately and spilled the fluid out. Some months later I was lolling victoriously in the sun. Whether that was good or bad I don't know; when I'm happy I think it was good, when I'm unhappy I think it was bad. But even when I'm miserable, I think I would have regretted not being born, since nothing is worse than nothingness. Let me say again: I'm not afraid of pain. We are born with pain; it grows with us, and we get used to it just as to the fact we have two arms and legs. Actually, I'm not even afraid of dying, dying means you at least were born, you escaped from nothingness. What I'm truly afraid of is nothingness, not being, never having existed, even by chance, by mistake, by the carelessness of others.

A lot of women ask themselves why they should bring a child into the world? So that it will be hungry, so that it will be cold, so that it will be betrayed and humiliated, so that it will be slaughtered by war or disease? They reject the hope that its hunger will be satisfied, its cold warmed, that loyalty and respect will accompany it through life, that it will devote a life to the effort to eliminate war and disease. Maybe they're right. But is nothingness preferable to suffering? Even when I weep over my failures, my disillusions, my torments, I am sure that suffering is preferable to nothingness. And if I extend this to life, to the dilemma of being born or not, every nerve in my body cries out that it is better to be born than not to be. But can I impose such reasoning on you? Doesn't that mean that I am bringing you into the world for myself alone and no one else? I'm not interested in bringing you into the world only for myself and no one else. I don't need you at all.

* * *

YOU'VE SENT ME NO ANSWERS, you've given no signs. And how could you? It's been too short a time: if I were to ask the doctor for confirmation of your existence he'd only smile. But I've decided for you: you will be born. I did so after seeing you in a photograph, a photograph of a three-week-old embryo, published in a magazine along with an article on the development of life. And while I was looking at it my fear went away as quickly as it had come. You looked like a mysterious flower, a transparent orchid. At the top one could make out a kind of head with the two protuberances that will become the brain. Lower down, a kind of cavity that will become the mouth. At three weeks you're almost invisible, the captions explain—about an eighth of an inch. Still, you're growing a suggestion of eyes, something resembling a spinal column, a nervous system, a stomach, a liver, intestines, lungs. Your heart is already present, and it's big: in proportion, nine times bigger than mine. It pumps blood and beats regularly from the eighteenth day on: how could I throw you away? What do I care if you only started out by chance or mistake? Didn't the world where we find ourselves also begin by chance and perhaps by mistake? Some people maintain that in the beginning there was nothing except a great calm, a great motionless silence; then came a spark, a split, and what had not been there before now was. The split was soon followed by others: unforeseen, insensate, forever unmindful of the consequences. And among the consequences bloomed a cell, it too by chance and perhaps by mistake, that was immediately multiplied by millions, by billions, until trees and fish and men were born. Do you think someone considered the dilemma before the spark? Do you think someone wondered whether that cell would like it or not? Do you think someone wondered about its hunger, its cold, its unhappiness? I doubt it. Even if that someone had existed—a God perhaps comparable to the beginning of the beginning, beyond time and space—he wouldn't have been concerned with good and evil. It all happened because it could happen, therefore had to happen, in accordance with the only arrogance that is legitimate. And the same thing goes for you. I take the responsibility of choice.

I take it without egoism, Child. I swear it gives me no pleasure to bring you into the world. I don't see myself walking in the street with a swollen belly, I don't see myself nursing you and bathing you and teaching you to talk. I'm a working woman and I have many other tasks and interests: I've already told you I don't need you. But I'll carry on with you, whether you like it or not. I'll impose upon you the same arrogance that was imposed on me, and on my mother, my grandmother, my grandmother's mother: all the way back to the first human born of another human being, whether he liked it or not. Probably, if he or she had been allowed to choose, he would have been frightened and answered: No, I don't want to be born. But no one asked their opinion, and so they were born and lived and died after giving birth to another human being who was not asked to choose, and that one did likewise, for millions of years, right down to us. And each time it was an arrogance without which we would not exist. Courage, Child. Don't you think the seed of a tree needs courage to break through the surface of the soil and sprout? A puff of wind is enough to break it, a rat's paw to crush it. Still it sprouts and stands firm and grows to scatter other seeds. And becomes part of a forest. If some day you cry, "Why did you bring me into the world, why?" I'll answer: "I did what the trees do and have done, for millions and millions of years before me. I thought it was the right thing."

I must not change my mind by remembering that human beings are not trees, that the suffering of a human being, since he's conscious, is a thousand times greater than that of a tree, that it does none of us any good to become a forest, that not all a tree's seeds generate new trees: the great majority are lost. Such an about-face is possible, Child: our logic is full of contradictions. The minute you state something, you see its opposite. And you even realize that the opposite is just as valid as what you'd stated. My reasoning today could be turned around with a snap of the fingers. In truth, I am already confused, disoriented. Maybe it's because I can't confide in anyone but you. I'm a woman who has chosen to live alone. Your father isn't with me. And I'm not sorry, even though my eyes so often stare at the door where he went out, with his determined step, without my trying to stop him, almost as though we had nothing to say to each other any more.

* * *

I'VE TAKEN YOU TO THE DOCTOR. It wasn't so much confirmation I wanted as some advice. His answer was to shake his head and tell me I'm impatient, he still can't say, and I should come back in two weeks prepared to discover that you're a product of my imagination. I'll go back just to show him he's an ignoramus. All his science is not worth my intuition; how can a man understand a woman who is expecting a child. He can't get pregnant . . . Is that an advantage or a limitation? Up until yesterday it seemed to me an advantage, even a privilege. Today it seems to me a limitation, even an impoverishment. There's something glorious about enclosing another life in your own body, in knowing yourself to be two instead of one. At moments you're even invaded by a sense of triumph, and in the serenity accompanying that triumph nothing bothers you: neither the physical pain you'll have to face, nor the work you'll have to sacrifice, nor the freedom you'll have to give up. Will you be a man or a woman? I'd like you to be a woman. I'd like for you one day to go through what I'm going through. I don't at all agree with my mother, who thinks it's a misfortune to be born a woman. My mother, when she's very unhappy, sighs: "Oh, if only I'd been born a man!" I know ours is a world made by men for men, their dictatorship is so ancient it even extends to language. *Man* means man and woman; *mankind* means all people; one says *homicide* whether it's the murder of a man or a woman. In the legends that males have invented to explain life, the first human creature is a man named Adam. Eve arrives later, to give him pleasure and cause trouble. In the paintings that adorn churches, God is an old man with a beard, never an old woman with white hair. And all heroes are males: from Prometheus who discovered fire to Icarus who tried to fly, on down to Jesus whom they call the Son of God and of the Holy Spirit, almost as though the woman giving birth to him were an incubator or a wet-nurse. And yet, or just for this reason, it's so fascinating to be a woman. It's an adventure that takes such courage, a challenge that's never boring. You'll have so many things to engage you if you're born a woman. To begin with, you'll have to struggle to maintain that if God exists he might even be an old woman with white hair or a beautiful girl. Then you'll have to struggle to explain that it wasn't sin that was born on the day when Eve picked an apple: what was born that day was a splendid virtue called disobedience. Finally, you'll have to struggle to demonstrate that inside your smooth shapely body there's an intelligence crying out to be heard. To be a mother is not a trade. It's not even a duty. It's only one right among many. What an effort it will be for you to convince others of this fact. You'll rarely be able to. And often, almost always, you'll lose. But you mustn't get discouraged. To fight is much better than to win, to travel much more beautiful than to arrive: once you've won or arrived, all you feel is a great emptiness. And to overcome that emptiness you have to set out on your travels again, create new goals. Yes, I hope you're a woman. And I hope you'll never say what my mother says. I've never said it.

* * *

But I'll be just as glad if you're born a man. Maybe more so, since you'll be spared many humiliations, much servitude and abuse. If you're born a man, you won't have to worry about being raped on a dark street. You won't have to make use of a pretty face to be accepted at first glance, of a shapely body to hide your intelligence. You won't have to listen to nasty remarks when you sleep with someone you like; people won't tell you that sin was born on the day you picked an apple. You'll have to struggle much less. And you'll be able to struggle more comfortably to maintain that if God exists he could even be an old woman with white hair or a beautiful girl. You'll be able to disobey without being derided, to love without fear of pregnancy, to take pride in yourself without being laughed at. But you'll run into other forms of slavery and injustice: life isn't easy even for a man, you know. You'll have firmer muscles, and so they'll ask you to carry heavier loads, they'll impose arbitrary responsibilities on you. You'll have a beard, and so they'll laugh at you if you cry and even if you need tenderness. You'll have a tail in front, and so they'll order you to kill or be killed in war and demand your complicity in perpetuating the tyranny that was set up in the caves. And yet, or just for this reason, to be a man will be an equally wonderful adventure, a task that will never disappoint you. If you're born a man, I hope you'll be the sort of man I've always dreamed of: kind to the weak, fierce to the arrogant, generous to those who love you, ruthless to those who would order you around. Finally, the enemy of anyone who tells you that the Jesuses are sons of the Father and of the Holy Spirit, not of the women who gave birth to them.

Child, I'm trying to tell you that to be a man doesn't mean to have a tail in front: it means to be a person. And to me, it's important above all that you be a person. *Person* is a marvelous word, because it sets no limits to a man or a woman, it draws no frontier between those who have that tail and those who don't. Besides, the thread dividing those who don't have it from those who do is such a thin one: in practice it's reduced to being able to grow another creature inside one's body or not. The heart and the brain have no sex. Nor does behavior. Remember that. And if you should be a person with heart and brains, I certainly won't be among those who will insist that you behave one way or another—as a male or female. I'll only ask you to take full advantage of the miracle of being born and never to give in to cowardice. Cowardice is a beast that is forever lurking. It attacks us all, every day, and there are very few people who don't let themselves be torn to pieces by it. In the name of prudence, in the name of expedience, sometimes in the name of wisdom. Cowardly as long as some risk is threatening them, humans become bold once the risk has passed. You must never avoid risk: even when fear is holding you back. To come into the world is already a risk. The risk of regretting later that you were born.

Maybe it's too soon to talk to you like this. Maybe I should keep silent for the moment about sad and ugly things and tell you about a world of innocence and gaiety. But that would be like drawing you into a trap, Child. It would be like encouraging you to believe that life is a soft carpet on which you can walk barefoot and not a road full of stones, stones on which you stumble, fall, injure yourself. Stones against which we must protect ourselves with iron shoes. And even that's not enough because, while you're protecting your feet, someone's always picking up a stone to throw at your head. I wonder what other people would say if they could hear me. Would they accuse me of being crazy or just cruel? I've looked at your last picture and, at five weeks, you're not quite half an inch long. You're changing a lot. Instead of a mysterious flower you now look like a very pretty larva, or rather a little fish that's rapidly putting out fins. Four fins that will turn into arms and legs. Your eyes are already two tiny black specks enclosed in a circle, and at the end of your body you have a little tail! The captions say that at this period it's almost impossible to distinguish you from the embryo of any other mammal: if you were a cat, you'd look more or less the way you do now. In fact you have no face. Not even a brain. I'm talking to you, Child, and you don't know it. In the darkness that enfolds you, you don't even know you exist: I could throw you away and you wouldn't even know I'd done so. You'd have no way of knowing whether I'd done you a wrong or a favor.

* * *

YESTERDAY I GAVE IN TO A BAD MOOD. You must excuse my talk about throwing you away. It was just talk, nothing more. My choice is still the same, though all around me it's cause for surprise. Last night I spoke with your father. I told him about you. I told him on the telephone because he's far away and, judging by what I heard, it wasn't exactly good news. First of all, I heard a deep silence, and we hadn't even been cut off. Then I heard a hoarse, stammering voice: "What will it take?" I didn't follow his meaning and answered, "Nine months, I guess. Or rather less than eight, now." And then the voice stopped being hoarse and became strident: "I'm talking about money." "What money?" I asked. "The money to get rid of it, of course." Yes, he actually said "get rid of it." As though you were a parcel. And when I explained to him, as calmly as possible, that I had quite other intentions, he went into a long argument in which pleading alternated with advice, advice with threats, and threats with flattery. "Think of your career, consider the responsibilities, one day you'll be sorry, what will other people say." He must have spent a fortune on that phone call. Every so often the operator came on in a bewildered tone to ask: "Are you still talking?" I was smiling, almost amused. But I was much less amused when he, encouraged by the fact that I was listening to him in silence, ended by saying that we could each pay half the expense: after all we were "both guilty." I suddenly felt nauseated. I was ashamed for him. And I hung up thinking that once I had loved him.

Loved him? One day you and I will have to have a little talk about this business called love. I still don't understand what it's all about. My guess is that it's just a gigantic hoax, invented to keep people quiet and diverted. Everyone talks about love: the priests, the advertising posters, the literati, and the politicians, those of them who make love. And in speaking of love and offering it is a panacea for every tragedy, they wound and betray and kill both body and soul. I hate this word, which you find everywhere, in every language. I-love-to-walk, I-love-to-drink, I-love-to-smoke, I-love-freedom, I-love-my-lover, I-love-my-child. I try never to use it. I don't even ask myself if what is troubling my heart and mind is this thing they call love. Indeed I don't know if I love you. I don't think of you in terms of love. I think of you in terms of life. As for your father, the more I think of it, the more I'm afraid I never loved him. Admired him yes, desired him yes, but loved no. The same goes for those who came before him, disappointing ghosts in a search that always failed. Failed? Not completely. It was worth something after all: to understand that nothing threatens your freedom as much as the mysterious rapture that a human being can feel toward another, a man toward a woman, for instance, or a woman toward a man. There are no straps or chains or bars that can hold you in a blinder slavery, a more desperate sense of helplessness. Beware of giving yourself to someone in the name of that rapture: it only means forgetting yourself, your rights, your dignity, and thus your freedom. Like a dog floundering in the water you try vainly to reach a shore that doesn't exist, a shore whose name is Loving and Being Loved, and you end in frustration, scorn, disillusionment. At best you end up wondering what drove you to throw yourself in the water: dissatisfaction with yourself, the hope of finding in another something you didn't see in yourself? Fear of solitude, of boredom, of silence? A need to possess and be possessed? According to some, that's love. But I'm afraid it's something much less: a hunger that, once satisfied, leaves you with a kind of indigestion. A wish to vomit. And yet, there must still be a way that would show me the meaning of this damned word, Child. There must still be a way for me to find out what it is and that it exists. I have such a hunger and need for it. And it's this need, this hunger, that leads me to think: maybe it's true, what my mother has always maintained, that love is what a woman feels for her child when she takes it in her arms and feels how alone, helpless, and defenseless it is. At least for as long as it remains helpless and defenseless, it doesn't insult you, doesn't disappoint you. What if you should be the one to make me discover the meaning of that absurd four-letter word? You who are robbing me of myself and sucking my blood and breathing my breath?

I can see a sign of it. Lovers enduring separation console themselves with photographs. And I always have your photographs in my hand. By now it's become an obsession. The minute I come home I seize that magazine, I calculate the days, your age, and I try to find you. Today you've completed six weeks. Here you are at six weeks, seen from the back. How cute you've become! No longer a fish, no longer a larva, no longer something formless, you already look like a human being: with that big bald pink head. The spinal column is well defined, a white strip securely in the middle. Your arms are no longer confused protuberances nor fins, but wings. You've grown wings! I am overcome by the wish to caress them, to caress you. What's it like there in the egg? According to the photographs, you're suspended in a transparent egg that looks like the glass egg in which one puts a rose. In place of the rose, you. From the egg extends a cord ending in a remote white ball, with veins of red and spots of blue. Seen in this way, it looks like the earth, observed from thousands and thousands of miles away. Yes, it's just as though an endless thread, as long as the idea of life, were extended from the earth, across that distance, to arrive at you. In such a logical, meaningful way. So how can they say human beings are an accident of nature?

The doctor told me to come back at the end of six weeks. I'm going tomorrow. And needles of anxiety pierce my soul, each alternating with a flush of joy.

* * *

In a tone wavering between the solemn and the cheerful, he lifted a sheet of paper and said: "Congratulations, Madam." Automatically I corrected him: "Miss." It was as though I'd given him a slap. Solemnity and cheerfulness disappeared, and staring at me with calculated indifference, he replied, "Ah!" Then he took his pen, crossed out *Mrs.*, and wrote *Miss.* Thus, in a cold, white room, through the voice of a man coldly dressed in white, Science gave me its official announcement that you existed. It made no impression on me, since I'd already known long before it did. But I was surprised that my marital status should be emphasized and that a correction had to be made on a sheet of paper. It smacked of a warning, a complication for the future. Even the way Science then told me to undress and lie down on the table was anything but cordial. Both the doctor and the nurse behaved as though I were somehow disagreeable to them. They didn't look me in the face. On the other hand, they exchanged meaningful looks. Once I was on the table, the nurse became upset because I hadn't spread my legs or put them in the two metal stirrups. Irritably she did it herself, saying, "Here, here!" I felt ridiculous and vaguely obscene. I was grateful to her when she covered my naked body with a towel. But the worst was when the doctor put on a rubber glove and angrily stuck his finger inside me. With his finger he pressed, he pried, he pressed again. Not only was he hurting me, I was afraid he wanted to crush you because I wasn't married. Finally he took his finger out and announced: "All's well, completely normal." He also gave me some advice, telling me that pregnancy is not an illness, it's a natural state; therefore, I should go on doing what I did before. It was important not to smoke too much, not to overexert myself, not to bathe in water that was too hot, not to consider any criminal decisions. "Criminal?" I asked, in astonishment. And he: "The law forbids it. Remember that!" To reinforce the threat he even prescribed some lutein pills and told me to come back every two weeks. He said it all without a smile, then told me to pay on the way out. As for the nurse, she didn't even say good-bye. And as she was closing the door, I had the impression that she shook her head disapprovingly.

We'll have to get used to such things, I'm afraid. In the world you're about to enter, and despite all the talk about changing times, an unmarried woman expecting a child is most often looked on as irresponsible. At best, as an eccentric, a troublemaker. Or a heroine. Never as a mother like the others. The druggist from whom I bought the lutein pills knows me and is well aware that I have no husband. When I gave him the prescription, he raised his eyebrows and stared at me with dismay. After the druggist, I went to the tailor, to order an overcoat. Winter is coming, and I want to keep you warm. With his mouth full of pins to fasten the cloth, the tailor began taking measurements. When I explained that he should make them generous because I was pregnant and would have a big stomach by the time winter came, he blushed violently. His jaw dropped and I was afraid he'd swallowed the pins. He hadn't, they had fallen on the floor. He also dropped his tape measure, and I felt sorry to have caused him such embarrassment. The same with my boss. Whether we like it or not, my boss is the one who buys my work and gives us money to live on: it would have been dishonest not to tell him that in a little while I wouldn't be able to work as before. So I went in his office and told him. He was speechless. Then he found his voice and stammered that he respected my decision, or rather admired me for it; he thought me very courageous, but it would be wiser not to talk about it to everyone. "It's one thing to talk between ourselves, we're worldly people, but another thing to say it to those who can't understand. And anyway you might change your mind, right?" He kept dwelling on the possibility of my changing my mind. At least up until the third month I had plenty of time to think about it, he kept repeating, and it would be a good idea to think about it: I was so well launched on my career, why interrupt it for sentimental reasons? It isn't a matter of interrupting my work for a few months or a year, it is a matter of changing the whole course of my life, he said. I'd no longer be so available, and I shouldn't forget that it was on my availability that the company had counted in launching me. Also, he said, he had so many fine projects in store for me. Should I reconsider, all I had to do was tell him. And he would help me.

Your father has telephoned a second time. His voice was trembling. He wanted to know if I'd had any confirmation. I told him yes. He asked me a second time when I would "get it taken care of." I hung up a second time without listening to him. What I can't understand is why, when a woman announces that she's legally pregnant, everybody starts making a fuss over her, taking the packages out of her hands, and begging her not to exert herself, to rest quietly. How wonderful, congratulations, sit down here, take a rest. With me they keep still, silent, or make speeches about abortion. I'd call it a conspiracy, a plot to separate us. And there are moments when I feel anxious, when I wonder who will win: we or they? Maybe it's because of that telephone call. It revived bitter thoughts that I hoped were forgotten, injuries I thought were overcome. The ones inflicted by those men before your father, those ghosts through whom I understood that love is a hoax. The wounds are healed, the scars barely visible, but a phone call is enough to make them ache again. Like old broken bones when the weather changes.

* * *

YOUR UNIVERSE IS THE EGG wherein you float, huddled up and almost devoid of weight, now six and a half weeks old. They call it the amniotic sac and the fluid that fills it is a saline solution that serves to cushion you against the force of gravity, to protect you from blows provoked by my movements, and also to feed you. Up until four days ago it was even your sole source of nourishment. By a complicated and almost unbelievable process, you swallowed one part of it, absorbed another, expelled still another, and produced it again. For the past four days, however, it's I who's become your source of nourishment: through the umbilical cord. So many things have happened in these days: I feel exalted and admire you when I think of it. The placenta has been strengthened, the number of your blood cells has increased, and everything goes forward at a mad pace: the structure of your veins is now visible. Your arteries, too, are perfectly visible, and the vein of the umbilical cord that brings you my oxygen and the chemical substances you need. What's more, you've developed a liver, you've sketched out all your internal organs: even your sex and your reproductive organs have begun to bloom! You already know whether you'll be a man or a woman. But what exalts me the most, Child, is that you've even made yourself a pair of hands. One can now see your fingers. And you also have a tiny mouth, with lips! You have the beginning of a tongue. You have the openings for twenty little teeth. You have eyes. So tiny, hardly more than half an inch, so light, a tenth of an ounce, and yet you have eyes! To me it seems almost impossible that all these things can happen in the span of a few weeks. It seems unreal. And yet the beginning of the world, when that cell and everything that is born and breathes and dies to be reborn again was formed, must have happened just as it's happening with you: in a swarming, a swelling, a proliferation of life, increasingly complicated, ever more difficult, ever more rapid and ordered and perfect. How hard you're working, Child! Who says you're sleeping, rocking quietly in your fluids? You never sleep, you never rest. Who says you're at peace amid a harmony of sounds arriving at your softly padded membrane? I'm sure that for you it's a continual rinsing, a continual pumping, panting, rustling, an explosion of brutal noises. Who says you're inert matter, little more than a vegetable that can be extirpated with a spoon? If I want to be free of you, they insist, now is the moment to do it. Or rather the moment begins now. In other words, I was to wait for you to become a human being with eyes and fingers and a mouth in order to kill you. Not before. Before, you were too small to be singled out and torn away. They are crazy.

* * *

My friend, a married woman, says I'm the one who's crazy. She's had four abortions in three years. She already has two children and for her it would have been inadmissible to have a third. Her husband earns little, she has a job she likes and can't do without, her mother-in-law takes care of the children and, poor thing, you can't ask her to open a kindergarten! It's all very well to be romantic but reality is something else, says my friend. Even chickens don't bring into the world all the babies they might: if a chick were hatched from every fertilized egg, the world would be a henhouse. Don't you know that lots of hens drink their eggs? Don't you know that they hatch them out only once or twice a year? And rabbits: do you know that some female rabbits eat the weakest in the litter so as to be able to nurse the others? Wouldn't it be better to eliminate them in the beginning than bring them into the world to eat or be eaten? In my opinion, it would be still better not to conceive them at all. But the minute I bring up that argument, she loses her temper. She answers that she took the pill, of course. It made her sick, but still she took it. Then one night she forgot, and hence the first abortion. With the probe, she tells me. I don't understand exactly what this probe is. A needle, I guess, that kills. On the other hand, I do understand that many women use it, knowing it can cause infinite suffering and even send them to prison.

Are you wondering why this is all I talk to you about these days? I don't know why. Maybe because others keep harassing me about it and hoping. Maybe because at a certain point I thought about it myself without realizing it. Maybe because I don't want to admit to anyone else a doubt that's poisoning my soul. Today the mere idea of killing you kills me, and still the thought occurs to me. I'm confused by that talk about the chickens. I'm confused by my friend's anger when I show her your picture and point out your eyes, your hands. She answers that to see them truly, your eyes, your hands, it would take more than a microscope. She yells that I'm living a fantasy, that I'm trying to rationalize my sentiments, my dreams. She even exclaimed: "So what about the tadpoles you take out of the pool in your garden so they won't become frogs and keep you up all night with their croaking?" I know. I go on mercilessly telling you about the infamies of the world you're getting ready to enter, about the daily horrors we commit, and I bring up concepts that are too complicated for you. But little by little I have a growing certainty that you understand these things because you know everything already. It began on the day that I was racking my brain trying to explain to you that the earth is round like your egg, the sea composed of water like that in which you float, and I didn't succeed in explaining what I meant. All of a sudden I was paralyzed by the realization that my effort was useless, that you knew everything already and much more than I, and now the suspicion of having guessed right never leaves me. If there's a universe in your egg, why shouldn't there also be thought? Hasn't it been said that the subconscious is the memory of an existence lived before coming into the world? Is it? Then tell me, you who know everything: when does life begin? Tell me, I beg you: has yours really begun? For how long? From the moment when the drop of light they call sperm pierced and split the cell? From the moment you developed a heart and began to pump blood? From the moment you grew a brain, a spinal column, and were on your way to assuming a human form? Or else is the moment still to come? Are you only a motor in the making? What wouldn't I give, Child, to break your silence, to penetrate the prison surrounding you and which I surround, what wouldn't I give to see you and hear your reply!

We surely make a strange couple, you and I. Everything in you depends on me and everything in me on you: if you get sick, I get sick; if I die, you die. But I can't communicate with you nor you with me. In what's perhaps your infinite wisdom, you don't even know my face, how old I am, what language I speak. You don't know where I come from, where I live, what I do in life. If you tried to imagine me, you would have no way of knowing whether I'm black or white, young or old, tall or short. And I'm still wondering whether you're a person or not. We are two strangers tied to the same destiny, two beings united in the same body, unknown to each other, distant.

* * *

I've slept badly and had pains in the lower part of the stomach: was that you? I kept thrashing around in bed, haunted in sleep by absurd nightmares. Your father was in one of them, and he was crying. I'd never seen him cry, I had no idea he was capable of it. His tears splashed heavily in the pool in my garden and the pool was full of endless gelatinous ribbons. Inside the ribbons were little black eggs that extended into a kind of tail: tadpoles. I paid no attention to your father. My one concern was to kill the tadpoles so they wouldn't become frogs and keep me awake all night with their croaking. The method was simple: all I had to do was lift the ribbons out with a stick and spread them on the lawn, where the sun would kill them by drying them out. But the ribbons were slippery and wriggled away, spiraling back rapidly into the water and sinking into the slime: I wasn't able to spread them on the grass. Then your father stopped crying and started helping me, and he had no trouble. He drew the ribbons out of the water with the branch of a tree, and they didn't slip away from him; he piled them on the grass. Calmly and systematically. And this made me suffer. Because it was like seeing dozens, hundreds of babies gasping and drying up in the sun. In my anguish, I tore the branch out of his hands, crying, "Let them alone! You were born, weren't you?"

In the other nightmare there was a kangaroo. It was a female kangaroo, and from her womb emerged a tender and living thing: a sort of delicate worm. It looked around bewildered, almost as though trying to understand where it was, then began climbing up the hairy body. It proceeded slowly, laboriously, slipping and falling, but finally it reached the pouch and with a final tremendous effort threw itself headlong inside. I realized it wasn't you; it was the embryo of the kangaroo, which is born this way because it emerges early from the prison of the egg and completes its formation outside the womb. But I spoke to it as though it were you. I thanked it for having come to show me that it wasn't a thing but a person. I told it that now we were no longer two strangers, two unknowns, and laughed happily. I laughed . . . But Grandmother arrived. She was very old and very sad. All the weight of the world seemed to press down on her curved shoulders. In her wasted hands she held a little doll with closed eyes and an oversized head. She said: "I'm so tired. I'm paying for the abortions. I've had eight children and eight abortions. If I'd been rich I'd have had sixteen children and not a single abortion. It's not true that you get used to it; every time is the first time. But the priest didn't understand this." The little doll was the size of a crucifix, the kind you carry in your pocket. Lifting it like a crucifix, Grandmother went into a church where she knelt down at a confessional and began to whisper something. From behind the grating a harsh voice rose, the voice of the priest: "You've killed a human being! You've killed a human being!" Grandmother was trembling for fear that others were listening. She kept imploring: "Don't shout, Father, I beg you! You'll get me arrested! I beg you!" But the priest didn't lower his voice, and Grandmother fled. She ran through the streets, followed by the police, and it was heartrending to see an old woman running like this. I felt as though I'd faint, and I was thinking: her heart will break, she's going to die. The police grabbed her at the door of her house. They took away the little doll and tied Grandmother's arms. She said proudly, "I'm sorry, but I'll do it again. I never do it willingly but I can't take care of so many children. I can't." I was awakened by those pains in the lower part of the stomach.

I must stop seeing my friend. It's her speeches that

cause me these nightmares. Last evening she invited me to supper: her husband was away; she thought it would be a good chance to talk to me about you, and it was torture. It seems indeed that there's a scientist, Dr. H. B. Munson, who's in agreement with her. Even the fetus, this man declares, is practically inert matter, little more than a vegetable that can be extirpated with a spoon. At most it can be considered a "coherent system of unrealized capacity." According to some biologists, on the other hand, the human being begins at the time of conception since the fertilized egg contains DNA: deoxyribonucleic acid composed of the proteins that form an individual. A thesis to which Dr. Munson replies that even the spermatozoa, even the unfertilized egg, contain DNA. Are we then to consider the egg and sperm as though they were human beings? Then there's a group of doctors for whom a human being becomes a human being after twenty-eight weeks, namely at the moment when it can survive outside the uterus even though gestation has not been completed. And there's a group of anthropologists for whom a human being is not even a newborn baby but someone who's been molded by cultural and social influences. We almost ended up in a quarrel. My friend favored the opinion of the anthropologists and I was prompted to accept that of the biologists. Irritated, she accused me of being on the side of the priests: "You're a Catholic, a Catholic, a Catholic!" I was offended. I'm not a Catholic, and she knows it. What's more, I deny that priests have any right to interfere in this matter, and she knows it. But I cannot, absolutely cannot, accept the arbitrary principles of Dr. Munson. I cannot, absolutely cannot, understand anyone who sticks a probe into herself as though taking a cathartic to eliminate undigested food. Unless . . .

Unless what? Am I going back on my decision? I seemed to be so sure of myself, to have triumphed so gloriously over all my uncertainties, all my doubts. Why do they come back to me now, under all these disguises? And by way of this malaise that makes my head spin, by way of these pains that stab me in the belly? I must be strong, Child. I must keep faith with myself and you. I must carry you to the end so that you'll grow up to be someone who resembles neither the priest who shouted in my dream, nor my friend and her Dr. Munson, nor the police who tied Grandmother's arms. The first considers you the property of God, the second the property of the mother, the third the property of the state. You belong neither to God nor the state nor me. You belong to yourself and no one else. After all you're the one who's taken the initiative. I was wrong to think I was imposing a choice on you. By keeping you, I'm only bowing to the command you gave me when your drop of life was ignited. I've chosen nothing; I've obeyed. If anyone is a victim, it's not you, Child: it's I. Isn't that what you want to tell me when you hurl yourself against my body like a vampire? Isn't that what you want to confirm when you give me nausea? I'm ill. All this week I've had trouble working. One of my legs is swollen. It would be awful if I had to give up that trip, which has already been set. And my boss seems to have understood that. In an almost threatening tone, he asked me today if I'd "be able to go," adding that he hoped so. It's an important assignment, one just right for me. He's eager about it, and so am I. If I weren't able to go . . . Of course I'll go. Didn't the doctor say that pregnancy is not an illness but a normal state, that I should go on doing what I've always done? You won't betray me.

* * *

SOMETHING HAS HAPPENED that I didn't foresee: the doctor has put me to bed. And here I am, motionless. I have to lie still and flat on my back. It's not easy, you understand, since I live alone: if someone rings the bell, I have to get up to open the door. And then I have to eat, I have to bathe. To fix myself some soup or go to the bathroom, I have to get out of bed, don't I? For the moment, my friend takes care of my meals. I gave her the keys and she comes by twice a day, poor thing. I exclaimed, "You didn't want a third child and here you're adopting a grown-up." She replied that better a grown-up than a newborn baby: you don't have to nurse it. Will you believe me when I say my friend is a good woman? She is. And not only because she comes here, but because she's stopped talking about that Munson, about her anthropologists. All of a sudden she seems very worried by the fear that I'll lose you. Don't be alarmed: there's no danger. The doctor repeated his examination and concluded that you're getting along fine; this immobility is a precaution due to the pains, which he attributes to different causes. You've completed two months, and two months mark a very delicate transition: the one in which the embryo becomes a fetus. You're forming bone cells, to take the place of the cartilage. You're extending your legs, just as a tree thrusts forth its branches, and toes are also emerging on your little feet. We'll have to be careful until the third month, and when that's over we can go back to our old habits; this business of lying still and flat on my back won't last more than two weeks. In fact, to the boss I pretended I'd had an attack of bronchitis. He believed me and assured me that the trip can wait after all: there are still a number of details to be arranged. Thank heaven for that; if he knew the truth, he might send someone else. Or go so far as to fire me. And that would be a fine situation, for me and for you: who would look after us? For one thing, there's been no sign of your father. I guess he doesn't want to get involved. Are you sorry? I'm not. The little I felt for him was extinguished by two phone calls. Or rather by the very fact that he talked to me on the phone instead of looking me in the face. On his return he could have come to see me, don't you think? He knows very well I wouldn't ask him to marry me, that I've never asked him, that I don't want to get married and would never want to: so what's keeping him? Do you suppose he feels guilty for having made love to me? One day Grandmother really went to confess and the priest gave her the following advice: "Don't go to bed with your husband, don't do it!" For some people, you know, the real sin of a man and a woman consists in making love in a bed. If you don't want children, they say, all you have to do is simply become chaste. All right, but since it's a bit difficult to decide who should be chaste and who not, let's all become chaste and transform ourselves into a planet of old people. Millions and millions of old people incapable of procreation, until the human race, as in science-fiction stories set on Mars, wipes itself out against a background of marvelous, crumbling cities inhabited only by ghosts. The ghosts of all those who might have existed and have not. The ghosts of children never born. Or else let's all become homosexuals, since the result would be the same: a planet of old people incapable of procreation, against a background of marvelous, crumbling cities, inhabited only by the ghosts of children never born. . . .

And if instead we were to make use of old people? Somewhere I've read that it's possible to effect the transplant of embryos. An achievement of biological technology. You remove the fertilized egg from the mother's womb and transfer it to the womb of another woman prepared to give it hospitality. There you let it grow. Look, if another woman were to give you hospitality—for instance, an old woman for whom lying motionless wouldn't constitute torture—you'd get born just the same and you wouldn't be here to torment me. Making babies is a job for old people anyway. They're so patient, old people. Would it offend you to be transplanted to a womb that's not mine? A good old womb that would never reproach you? And why should you be offended? I wouldn't be denying you life. I'd just be giving you another lodging. Forgive me. I'm raving. The trouble is that this immobility gets on my nerves, it brings out the worst in me.

* * *

TODAY I HAD A PLEASANT SURPRISE. The bell rang; I got up grumbling, and it was the postman with an airmail package. My mother had sent it, along with a letter signed by her and my father. I had told them about you some days ago. I thought it was my duty. And every morning I'd been anxiously expecting their answer, shuddering at the thought of the harsh or painful things they might write. They're two old-fashioned people, you see. Instead, their letter says that even though they feel shocked and upset, they rejoice all the same and welcome you. "We're two old dry trees by now, we have nothing more to teach you. Now it's you who has something to teach us. And if you've decided on it, that means it's right. We're writing to tell you that we accept your lesson." After reading the letter, I opened the package. Inside was a little plastic box, and inside that a pair of little white shoes. Tiny, tiny, so light, and white. Your first shoes. I can hold them on the palm of one hand, and they don't even cover it. And I get a lump in my throat when I touch them; my heart dissolves. You'll like my mother. With her you'll have two mothers and that will be true riches. You'll like her because she thinks that without children the world would end. You'll like her because she's large and soft, with a large, soft lap to sit on, two large, soft arms for protection, and a laugh that rings like a concert of little bells. I've never understood how she's able to laugh like that, but I think it's because she's cried a lot. Only those who have cried a lot can appreciate life in all its beauty and have a good laugh. It's easy to cry, hard to laugh. It won't take you long to learn this truth. Your encounter with the world will be a desperate wail; all you'll be able to do at first will be to cry. Everything will make you cry: light, hunger, anger. Weeks will go by, months, before your mouth opens in a smile, before your throat gurgles out a laugh. But you mustn't get discouraged. And when the smile comes, when the laugh comes, you must give it to me: to show me that I did the right thing by not availing myself of biological technology and handing you over to the womb of a mother more generous and patient than myself.

* * *

I've cut out the photograph that shows you at exactly two months: a close-up of your face enlarged forty times. I've pinned it to the wall, and lying here in bed I'm admiring it: haunted by your eyes. They're so large compared to the rest of your body, so wide open. What do they see? The water and nothing else? The walls of the prison and nothing else? Or what I can see too? I have a delightful and disturbing suspicion: the suspicion that they see through me. It makes me sad to think that soon you'll close them. On the edges of your eyelids a sticky substance is forming that in a few days will glue them together, to protect the pupils during their final development. You won't raise your eyelids again until the sixth month. For twenty weeks you'll live in complete darkness. What a pity! Or is it? With nothing to look at, you'll hear me better. I still have so much to tell you, and these days of immobility give me plenty of time, since my only activity is to read or watch television. And then I have to prepare you for a few uncomfortable truths. I can't really believe that you know everything already. But explaining these things to you will be difficult because your mind, if it exists, is acting on matters too different from the ones you'll find. In there you're alone, magnificently alone. Your only experience is yourself. We, instead, are many. Millions, billions. Each of our experiences depends on others, each of our joys, our sorrows, and . . .

Yes, that's were I'll begin. I'll begin by telling you that out here you'll no longer be alone, and should you want to free yourself from others, from their unwanted company, you'll never succeed. Out here one can't look after oneself all alone, as you're doing. Those who try go mad. At best, they fail. Sometimes someone does try. And escapes to the forest or sea swearing that he doesn't need the others, that the others will never find him again. But they find him. He may even be the one to come back. And he comes back defeated, to be part of the ant heap, the treadmill: in the desperate and impossible hope of finding his freedom there. You'll hear a lot of talk about freedom. It's a word we exploit almost as much as the word *love*, the most exploited word of all. You'll meet men who get themselves cut to pieces for freedom, undergoing tortures and even accepting death. And I hope you'll be one of them. But in the same moment that you get yourself tortured for freedom, you'll discover that freedom doesn't exist, that at most it existed only insofar as you sought it: like a dream, an idea born from the memory of your life before birth, when you were free because you were alone. Yes, I go on repeating that you're a prisoner in there; I can't help thinking how little room you have and that from now on you'll even be in darkness. But in that darkness, that little space, you're freer than you'll ever be in this huge and ruthless world. In there, you don't have to ask for anyone's permission, anyone's help, since you have no one alongside you and don't know what slavery is. Outside, you'll have countless masters. And the first will be myself who, without wishing it, maybe without knowing, will impose things on you that are right for me but not for you. Those nice little shoes, for instance. To me they're nice, but to you? You'll yell and scream when I put them on you. They'll bother you, I'm sure. But I'll put them on all the same, even telling you you're cold, and little by little you'll get used to them. You'll yield and be tamed, to the point of suffering when you don't have them on. And this will be the beginning of a long chain of servitude whose first link will always be represented by me, since you won't be able to do without me. I who will feed you, I who will cover you, I who will bathe you, I who will carry you in my arms. Later you'll start walking by yourself, eating by yourself, choosing for yourself where to go and when to wash. But then other forms of slavery will arise. My advice. My instructions. My recommendations. Your very fear of hurting me by doing things other than those I taught you. A lot of time will pass, in your eyes, before I let you leave like the bird whose parents throw it out of the nest the day it learns to fly. But finally that time will come, and I'll let you go, I'll let you cross the street alone, with the green light and with the red. I'll push you on. But this will do nothing to increase your freedom since you'll remain chained to me by the bondage of sentiments, the bondage of regret. Some call it the bondage of the family. I don't believe in the family. The family is a lie constructed the better to control people, the better to exploit their obedience to rules and legends, by whoever organized this world. We rebel more easily when we're alone; we resign ourselves more easily when living with others. The family is nothing but the mouthpiece for a system that cannot let you disobey, and its sanctity is nonexistent. All that exists are groups of men, women, and children compelled to bear the same name and live under the same roof, often hating and detesting each other. But regret exists, and the bonds exist, rooted in us like trees that bend not even to the hurricane, and they're as unavoidable as hunger and thirst. You can never free yourself from them, try as you may with all your will and logic. You may even think you've forgotten them, but one day they reemerge, incurably, mercilessly, to put the rope around your neck more tightly than any hangman. And to strangle you.

Along with that bondage, you'll know the kind imposed by others, namely by the thousands and thousands of inhabitants of the ant heap. Their habits, their laws. You have no idea how suffocating it is to imitate their habits, to respect their laws. Don't do this, don't do that, do this and do that... And if this is bearable when you live among decent people who have some idea of freedom, it becomes hell when you live among the arrogant who deny you even the luxury of dreaming of freedom, of realizing it in your imagination. The laws of the arrogant have only one advantage to offer: you can react to them by struggling and dying. The laws of decent people offer no escape since you've been persuaded that it's noble to accept them.

No matter what system you live under, there is no escaping the law that it's always the strongest, the cruelest, the least generous who win. Least of all can you escape the law that to eat you need money, to sleep you need money, to walk in a pair of shoes you need money, to keep warm in winter you need money, and to have money you have to work. They'll tell you a lot of stories about the necessity of work, the joy of work, the dignity of work. Don't ever believe it. It's just one more lie invented for the convenience of whoever organized this world. Work is blackmail and remains such even when you like it. You always work for someone, never for yourself. You always work with effort, never with joy. And never in the moment you would have liked. Even if you depend on no one and cultivate your own patch of earth, you still must hoe when the sun and the rain and the seasons tell you to. Even if you have no one to obey and can freely ply your own trade, you still must yield to the requirements and tyranny of others. Maybe in a very distant past, so distant that the memory of it has been lost, things were not this way. And working was a feast, a joy. But then there were only a few people, and so they were left alone. You're coming into the world one thousand nine hundred and seventy-five years after the birth of a man they call Christ, who himself came into the world hundreds of thousands of years after the first man whose name is unknown; and ever since then things have gone as I've told you. According to a recent statistic, there are already four billion of us. You're going to enter this heap. And then you will look back and wish for your solitary splashing in the water, Child!

* * *

I've written three fairy tales for you. I haven't really written them since I'm lying flat on my back and cannot write; so I shall simply tell them to you. Once upon a time there was a little girl who was in love with a magnolia tree. The magnolia stood in the middle of a garden. The little girl used to look at it for days on end, leaning out of the window from the top floor of a house facing on that garden. The little girl was very small, and to look down at the magnolia she had to climb on a chair, where her mother used to find her and cry out, "Oh God, she'll fall, she'll fall out the window!" It was a big magnolia, with big branches and big leaves and big flowers which opened like clean handkerchiefs and which no one picked because they were too high. As the little girl watched, day after day, the flowers would bloom, turn yellow, wither and fall to the ground with a small thud. And each day the little girl dreamed that someone would appear and pick a flower while it was still white. It was in this expectation that she stayed at the window, her arms resting on the sill and her chin resting on her arms. There were no other houses around her, only a wall rising steeply at the side of the garden and ending in a terrace where washing was hung out to dry. You knew when it was dry because of the way it slapped in the wind, whereupon a woman would arrive to collect it all in a basket and take it away. But one day the woman arrived and, instead of collecting the wash, she too began looking at the magnolia: it was almost as though she was trying to see if she could pick a flower. She stood there a long time staring at the tree while the laundry flapped in the wind. Then she was joined by a man who put his arms around her. She put her arms around him too, and soon they fell down on the terrace together and lay gasping together for a long time and finally went to sleep. The little girl was surprised; she couldn't understand why the two of them lay sleeping on the terrace instead of looking at the magnolia and trying to pick a flower, and she was waiting patiently for them to wake up when another man appeared. He was very angry. He said nothing, but it was clear that he was very angry because he immediately flung himself on the two of them. First on the man, who jumped up and ran away, then on the woman, who began running through the hanging wash. He ran after her, trying to catch her, and in the end he did. He lifted her up as though she weighed nothing and threw her off the terrace: onto the magnolia. It seemed to take a long time for the woman to reach the magnolia, but when she did, she landed on the branches with a loud crack as if a branch had broken. At that moment the woman grabbed at a flower and plucked it. She stayed there motionless with her flower in her hand. Then the little girl called her mother. She said: "Mama, they threw a woman down on the magnolia and she picked a flower." Her mother came, screamed that the woman was dead, and from that day on the little girl grew up convinced that if a woman picked a flower she must die.

I was that little girl. May God protect you from learning the way I learned that it is always the strongest, the cruelest, the least generous who wins. God keep you from understanding as early as I did that a woman is the first to pay for this reality. But it is a mistake for me to hope that. It is better to hope that you'll soon lose this virginity called childhood. It's an illusion. From now on you must prepare to defend yourself, to be quicker and stronger, and to throw others down from the terrace. Especially if you're a woman. This too is a law: unwritten but obligatory. It's either you or me, either I save myself or you save yourself: these are the terms of this law. And beware of forgetting it. Everybody does harm to somebody, here among the living, Child. Those who don't, succumb. And don't listen to those who say that it's the better who succumb. It's the weaker who succumb, and they're not necessarily the better. I've never pretended that women are better than men, that because of their goodness they deserve not to die. To be good or bad doesn't count: life out in this world doesn't depend on that. It depends on a relation of forces based on violence. And survival is violence. You'll wear leather shoes because someone has killed a cow and skinned it to make leather. You'll warm yourself with a fur coat because someone has killed an animal, a hundred animals, to strip away the fur. You'll eat chicken livers because someone has killed a chicken that was doing harm to no one. Perhaps not to no one, because even that chicken was devouring little worms that went around peacefully nibbling plants. There's always someone who eats or skins another to survive: from men to fish. Even the fishes eat each other, the bigger ones swallow the smaller. The same for the birds, the insects, anything. I believe it is only trees and plants that devour no one: they nourish themselves on water, sun, and nothing else. At times, however, deprived of sun and water, they wither and die. But is now the time for you to know these horrors, you who live and nourish and warm yourself without killing anybody?

* * *

HERE IS A SECOND FAIRY TALE. Once upon a time there was a little girl who was very fond of chocolate. But the more she liked chocolate, the less chocolate she had. This was because she had once been given as much chocolate as she wanted. During that time she lived in a house filled with light that came in through the windows. Then one day she woke up and there was no sky and no light and no chocolate. From the windows of her new room, which were placed almost at the ceiling and protected by a prison grating, all she could see were feet going back and forth. She could also see dogs, and at first it was fun because you could see the whole dog, including the head. But then the dogs lifted their legs and made peepee on the grating, while the little girl's mother wept: "Oh, no, not that!" Her mother was always weeping, especially when she looked at her big stomach, which made her apron stick out, and spoke to it: "You couldn't have picked a worse moment!" At which point the little girl's father began to cough in his bed, a cough that left him as though dead when it subsided. Her father stayed in bed even during the day, his face yellow and his eyes shining. And sad. As the little girl reckoned it, the end of the chocolate had come at the same time as her father's illness and the move to this house with neither sky nor joy. They had no money.

In order to get money, the little girl's mother went to clean house for a beautiful lady whom she called by her first name and who called her by hers. She was a rich aunt and was always changing her clothes. They even said she had a purse for every dress and a pair of shoes for every purse. Her house was on the river and all the sky in the city came in through the windows. But still the beautiful lady wasn't happy. She was always complaining: because a hat didn't look right, or because her cat sneezed, or because her maid had been away in the country for a month and showed no signs of returning. So the little girl's mother took the place of this irresponsible maid. Every day, from nine to one, she left her husband and took the little girl with her, insisting it was better for her to get some air than to stay alongside a man with a punctured lung. They went by foot, a long distance through endless streets. As they walked, her mother kept wondering aloud at what unhappiness she would hear about this time from the beautiful lady, and then, before ringing the bell, she would whisper, "Cheer up!" The sound of the bell was answered by a languid voice, followed by an even more languid step, and the door opened on a dressing gown that went all the way down to the feet: sometimes white, sometimes pink, sometimes blue. They trod on carpets as they entered, and the little girl's mother placed her on a stool, almost as though she were a package. She told her to be quiet and still and not to bother anyone, then disappeared into the kitchen to wash the dishes. The beautiful lady by then was stretched out on a divan, reading the newspaper and smoking with a cigarette holder. Clearly she had nothing else to do. And the little girl couldn't understand why she didn't wash the dishes herself, instead of having them washed by her mother who had a big stomach.

That morning the beautiful lady's complaints had to do with money. She had begun while the little girl's mother was washing the dishes and she kept it up while she was cleaning the drawing room. "Don't you see?" she repeated. "That's all the money he wants to give me." And when the little girl's mother replied, "With all that money I'd feel like a princess," the lady got angry. She said, "To me it's barely enough for taxis. You don't mean to compare yourself to me!" The little girl's mother blushed, and with the excuse of brushing the rug she knelt on the floor and hid her face. The little girl felt a lump in her throat. And the tears burning in her eyes were just about to flow when her attention was caught by some golden objects glittering in the sun: a glass container for sweets, filled with chocolates. But not just ordinary chocolates: chocolates two or three times as big as those she'd been accustomed to eat in those faraway days in the house with the sky. Indeed, all of a sudden, the lump in her throat disappeared, to be replaced by a liquid that had the taste of chocolate. Her mother realized it. She gave her a terrible look to warn her: you ask for anything and you'll be sorry! The little girl understood and with dignity began gazing at the ceiling. She was gazing at the ceiling when the beautiful lady got up and, murmuring with boredom, went onto the balcony where she stood rubbing her wrist. The balcony faced out over a second, larger balcony. And on the second balcony were two rich children. The little girl knew this because she had once seen them and had understood they were rich because they were beautiful. They had the same beauty as the lady. Still rubbing her wrist, the lady ran to the edge. Enraptured, she smiled, leaned over to call them: *"Bonjour, mes petits pigeons! Ça va, aujourd'hui?"* And then: *"Attendez, attendez! Il y a quelque chose pour vous!"* She came back into the house, took the glass container, uncovered it, and, holding it daintily carried it onto the balcony and began to throw down chocolates. She threw them, saying: "Chocolates for my little pigeons! Chocolates for my little pigeons!" She threw more than half of them, amid bursts of laughter, and finally brought the container back to the table and took out one more chocolate. Slowly she stripped away the gold foil, held it for a moment, thinking of something or other, then ate it. While the little girl watched.

From that day on I've been unable to eat chocolate. If I eat it, I throw up. But I hope you'll like chocolate, Child, because I want to buy you a lot of it. I want to cover you with chocolate: to let you eat it for me till you're sick of it, till the sense of injustice that weighs on me so heavily is finally lifted. You'll come to know injustice as well as violence; that's something else you must get ready for. And not the injustice of killing a chicken to eat it, a cow to skin it, a woman to punish her: I mean the injustice that separates the haves from the have-nots. The injustice that leaves this poison in the mouth, while the pregnant mother brushes someone else's carpet. How this problem can be solved, I don't know. All those who have tried have only succeeded in replacing the one who brushes the carpet. Under whatever system you're born, whatever ideology, there's always someone brushing another's carpet.

There's always a little girl humiliated by a desire for chocolate. You'll never find a system or ideology that can change the hearts of men and erase their iniquity. When someone tells you with-us-it's-different, answer him: Liar. Then challenge him to demonstrate that with them there's no such thing as meals for the rich and meals for the poor, houses for the rich and houses for the poor, seasons for the rich and seasons for the poor. Winter is a season for the rich. If you're rich, the cold becomes a game because you buy a fur coat and heat your house and go skiing. If, instead, you're poor, the cold becomes a curse and you learn to hate even the beauty of a white, snow-covered landscape. Equality, Child, like freedom, exists only where you are now. Only as an egg and in the womb are we all equal. Is it really time for you to come to know of these injustices, you who live there and serve no one?

* * *

I DON'T KNOW IF THIS ONE IS A FAIRY TALE, but I'll tell it to you anyway. Once upon a time there was a girl who believed in tomorrow. Indeed everyone was always teaching her to believe in tomorrow, assuring her that tomorrow is always better. The priest assured her when he intoned his promises in church and announced the Kingdom of Heaven. The school assured her when it taught her that humanity goes forward: that once man lived in caves, then in unheated houses, then in houses with central heating. Her father assured her when he gave her examples from history and maintained that the mighty are always brought low. The girl lost faith in the priest fairly early. His tomorrow was death, and the girl was not at all interested in living beyond death in a luxurious hotel called the Kingdom of Heaven. She lost faith in the school a little later, during a winter when her hands and feet were covered with chilblains and sores. It was a great thing, to be sure, that men had progressed from caves to central heating, but her house had no central heating. She continued, however, to have a blind faith in her father. Her father was a courageous and stubborn man. For twenty years he had fought certain arrogant men dressed in black, and every time they cracked his skull, he said, courageously and stubbornly: "Tomorrow will come." There was a war in those years, and the arrogant men dressed in black seemed to be winning it. But her father shook his head and said, courageously and stubbornly: "Tomorrow will come."

The girl believed him because of what she had seen one night in July. On that night the arrogant men had been driven out and it seemed that their war was over, making way for tomorrow. But September came and the arrogant men returned, with new ones who spoke German. The war was redoubled. The girl felt she had been betrayed. She asked her father, who answered, "Tomorrow will come." And he convinced her by showing her that tomorrow could not be far off because they were no longer alone: friends were arriving, a whole army of friends who were called allies. Next day the girl's city was bombarded by the friends who were called allies and a bomb fell right in front of her house. The girl was bewildered. If they were friends, why did they bomb her house? Her father replied that unfortunately they had to but that this in no way diminished their friendship, and the better to convince her he brought into the house two of those who had dropped the bombs. The "friends" had been taken prisoner by the arrogant men, but they had escaped. It was necessary to help them, her father explained, since tomorrow was their common cause. The girl agreed. Together with her father, who was risking the firing squad for these men, she hid the friends and fed them and guided them to safe villages. Then she settled down to wait for the army that was to bring the tomorrow. Weeks passed, months, and the army didn't come. And meanwhile people were dying under the bombs, the tortures, the shootings: the famous tomorrow now seemed only a dream made of dreams. Then the girl's father was arrested, beaten, tortured. The girl visited him in prison and could hardly recognize him, he had been so tortured. But even in prison, after being tortured, he said: "Tomorrow will come. A tomorrow without humiliation."

And in the end, the tomorrow arrived. It was an August dawn and during the night the city had been shaken by dreadful explosions. The bridges and streets had been blown up, and more innocent people had been killed. But then the dawn had emerged, splendid as the bells of Easter, and it brought the army of friends. Handsome, smiling, joyous, they advanced, angels in uniform, and people ran up to them throwing flowers and shouting their thanks. The girl's father, now freed, was greeted by everyone with great deference and in his eyes shone the light of one who has known the faith. Then somebody came up and told him to run to the allied command: something very serious had happened. The girl's father ran, wondering what this very serious thing could be. At the command post was a man who lay sobbing on the ground, his face buried in the grass. He must have been about thirty years old. He was wearing a blue suit, obviously chosen to welcome the friends, and in the buttonhole of the jacket there was a big red paper rose. In front of him, or rather over him, his legs spread, stood an angel in uniform with a machine gun slung on his shoulder. The girl's father bent over the man: "What have you done?" The man only sobbed more and whimpered, "Mama, mama, mama." The girl's father asked to speak to the allied commander. As the commander received him, he lifted his sharp face, adorned with carrot-colored mustaches, and waved a riding crop. "Are you one of the so-called representatives of the people?" The girl's father said yes. "Then let me inform you that your people have welcomed us by stealing. That man is a thief." The girl's father asked what he had stolen. "A haversack full of food and documents," the commander hissed. The girl's father asked what documents. "The leave papers of the sergeant who owns the haversack," the commander hissed. The girl's father asked if the papers had been recovered. "Yes, but torn!" the commander hissed. The girl's father suggested that perhaps they could be mended. And the food? Had that also been recovered? "The food has been eaten! A whole day's ration!" the commander shouted in fury. The girl's father checked a smile. He answered that this was indeed disagreeable: as a representative of the people he would take charge of the thief and order him to reimburse the sergeant for his losses. Then the riding crop traced a great spiral in the air and the commander replied that in his army thieves were shot. He ordered the girl's father to get out. Outside, the thief was still crying with his face buried in the grass: "Mama, mama, mama." The angel in uniform was still standing over him, his legs spread and the machine gun pointed. The legs were squat and hairy; the machine gun was aimed at the back of the man's neck. As she walked by, the girl heard a metallic click. The click of the safety catch when it is released.

The girl never found out if the thief had been executed, but from that day on she was always suspicious of the word *tomorrow*. And since her mind had connected the word *tomorrow* with the word *friends*, from that day on she was also suspicious of friends. After the British army came the American army. Everyone said the Americans would be kinder and more cordial, and the girl hoped this was true since many of them gave great bursts of laughter brimming with humanity. But she soon realized that even with their great bursts of laughter and humanity, they too raped and corrupted and behaved like masters; the famous tomorrow was only a new fear. And the hunger was the same. To appease their hunger, some women prostituted themselves; others washed clothes for the new masters. Every terrace, every courtyard was a showplace for hanging uniforms and socks and undershirts, a boast by those who were doing the most washing. Six pairs of socks, a loaf of American bread. Three undershirts, a can of pork and beans. One uniform, two cans of meat. The girl's father wouldn't allow his wife and daughter to touch those dirty clothes. He said that for better or worse the tomorrow had begun and must be defended with dignity. And to prove it, he invited some of the "friends" for a meal and gave them his ration of fresh food. One evening he even gave them his gold watch and delivered a fine speech recalling the prisoners he had aided for the tomorrow that was still their common cause. The friends took the gold watch and, in reply, offered to let his family wash clothes. The girl felt offended. But hunger is a beast full of temptations: a few days later, without telling her father, she thought about it and asked to wash the clothes. Two bags arrived. One contained dirty clothes and the other food. The one with food got opened at once and out came three cans of pork and beans, two loaves of bread, a jar of peanuts, and a whole bottle of strawberry jelly. The one with dirty clothes got opened later. And when the girl dumped it in the sink, she flushed with anger. They were all dirty underpants.

It was while washing the dirty underpants of others that I realized it: our tomorrow hadn't come and perhaps never would. We would always be deceived by promises: in a rosary of disappointments lightened by false consolations, pitiful gifts, wretched comforts to keep us quiet. Will my tomorrow ever come for you? I doubt it. It's been hundreds and thousands of years, and people are still bringing children into the world trusting in some tomorrow, hoping that tomorrow their children will live better lives than themselves. And that better life ends up at best with the acquisition of a miserable central heating system. Central heating is a fine thing when you're cold, but it can't give you happiness or protect your dignity. Even with central heating you still have to endure arrogance, afflictions, blackmail, and the tomorrow remains a lie. I told you in the beginning that nothing is worse than nothingness, that grief should not arouse fear, not even the fear of dying, because if one dies it means one was born. I told you it's always worthwhile to be born, since the alternative is silence and the void. But was that right, Child? Is it right for you to be born to die under a bomb or the rifle of a hairy soldier whose mess ration you've stolen out of hunger? The more you grow, the more frightened I become. The enthusiasm with which I rejoiced in the beginning has almost completely disappeared; I have lost the glorious certainty of having plucked the truth of life. I am more and more consumed by doubt. A doubt that rises and falls like the tide, now covering the beach of your existence in waves, now retreating and leaving only debris. Believe me, I'm not trying to discourage you or induce you not to be born: I only want to divide my responsibility with you and clarify yours for you. You still have time to consider, or rather to reconsider. As far as I'm concerned, be it high tide or low tide, I'm ready. But you? I've already asked you if you're ready to see a woman flung down on a magnolia tree, to watch chocolate being rained down on those who don't need it. Now I ask if you're ready to run the risk of washing the underpants of others and discovering that tomorrow is a yesterday. You for whom every yesterday is tomorrow, and every tomorrow a conquest. You still don't know the worst of realities: the world changes and remains the same.

* * *

TEN WEEKS. You're growing with amazing rapidity. Two weeks ago you measured less than an inch and a quarter and weighed just over a tenth of an ounce. Now you measure two and a half inches and weigh almost three-tenths of an ounce. You're all there. Nothing is left of the tiny little fish but the fact that you inhale and exhale fluid through your lungs. Your human skeleton is formed, with bones replacing the cartilage. Your ribs are cementing themselves at their ends almost as though your body were being buttoned up like an overcoat. And your egg, though expanding, is becoming more and more confining. Soon you'll find it uncomfortable. You'll toss around, you'll stretch, your arms and legs will make their first movements. Here you'll strike with your elbow, there with your knee. That's what I'm waiting for. The first blow will be a sign, an assent. I did the same when I told my mother not to drink any more medicine. And so she threw it away. But my hope diminishes as you grow: the faster you grow, the more I feel my hope slipping away. It reminds me of the friendly army that took so long to arrive. It's all because of this immobility. Two motionless weeks in bed are too much for me. How do women do it who have to lie in bed even seven or eight months? Are they women or larvae? The only point I agree on is that it does help. The cramps, the stabbing pains below the stomach, have gone. The nausea has gone, and my leg isn't swollen any more. But it's been replaced by a kind of fatigue, an anxiety that's like anguish. Where does it come from? Maybe from inactivity, boredom. I've never known inactivity, never had to put up with boredom. I can't wait for these last two days to be over—you'd think they were two years. This morning I quarreled with you. Are you offended? I was seized by a kind of hysteria. I told you that I too had my rights, that no one was entitled to forget it and that meant you as well. I shouted that I was exasperated with you, that I couldn't go on. Are you listening? Ever since I've known that you've closed your eyes, I have a feeling that you're not paying attention to what I tell you, that you're cradling yourself in a sort of unawareness. Come on, wake up. You don't want to? All right then, come here, next to me. Rest your little head on this pillow; we'll sleep together, our arms around each other. You and me, me and you . . . no one else will ever get into our bed.

* * *

HE'S COME. I never thought he would. It was in the evening, the key turned in the lock, and I thought it was my friend. Usually it's she who comes up to see me before supper. In fact I called out hello to her, expecting to see her come in panting with her little package: excuse-me-I'm-in-a-hurry-I've-brought-you-a-little-cold-meat-and-some-fruit-see-you-tomorrow. Instead it was he. He must have tiptoed in. I turned and there he was, tight-lipped and with a bunch of flowers in his hand. The first thing I felt was a pang in the belly. Not the usual knife stab but a pang: almost as though you were frightened to see him and had grasped me with your fists to take shelter and hide behind my womb. Then I couldn't breathe and felt benumbed by an icy wave. Did you feel it too? Did it hurt you? He was standing there in silence, with his tight-lipped expression and his flowers. I hated his face and his flowers. Why should he descend on us this way, like a thief in the night? Doesn't he know that pregnant women are supposed to avoid sudden stress? "What do you want?" I asked him. He put the flowers on the bed, in silence. I removed them immediately, saying that flowers on the bed bring bad luck, you put flowers on deathbeds. I put them on the night table. They were yellow flowers, clearly bought at the last moment, with no care and no sincerity. He stood quiet and still, a tall, dark shadow against the white of the walls. But he wasn't looking at me. He was looking at your photograph on the wall: the one showing you at two months, enlarged forty times. You could almost say he couldn't tear his eyes away from yours; and the more he looked at you, the more his head sank between his shoulders. Finally he covered his face with his hands and burst into tears. Softly at first, without making any noise. Then louder. He even sat down on the bed so as to cry more comfortably, and at each of his sobs the bed shook. I was afraid it would disturb you. "You're shaking the bed. The vibrations are bad for it," I said. He took his hands from his face, dried his eyes with a handkerchief, and went to sit in a chair. The one under your photograph. It was strange to see you both together. You with your steady, mysterious pupils, he with his flickering pupils, devoid of secrets. Then he said: "It's mine too."

Rage overwhelmed me. I sat up in bed and shouted at him that you were neither mine nor his: you were your own. I shouted that I detested this melodramatic rhetoric, this silliness from popular songs, and that I was supposed to stay quiet, under doctor's orders. What had he come here for, to kill you without an abortion so as to save money? I even slammed the bunch of flowers against the night table: three or four times, until the petals came off and fluttered in the air like confetti. When I fell back on the pillows I was perspiring so much that my pajamas stuck to my skin, and the pain in my womb was so bad I could hardly bear it. Still he didn't move. He bowed his head and murmured, "How can you treat me like this? How can you be so cruel?" He then began a long harangue centering on the fact that I was wrong, that you were both mine and his, that he'd thought about it so much, suffered so much, that for two months he'd been torturing himself over you, that he'd finally understood how noble and right my choice was, that a child should never be got rid of because a-child-is-a-child-not-a-thing. Then more banalities. I interrupted him. "You don't have it inside your body, you don't have to carry it inside your body for nine months." And his jaw dropped in surprise: "I thought you wanted it, that you were doing this willingly."

Then something happened that even I don't understand: I started to cry. I had never cried, you know, and I didn't want to, because it was humiliating and made me ugly. But the more I tried to hold back the tears, the more they gushed out, almost as though something inside me had broken. I even tried to light a cigarette. But the tears wet the cigarette. And so your father left the chair and came toward me and timidly caressed my head. Then he murmured, "I'll make some coffee," and went into the kitchen. When he came back, I'd regained control of myself. But he had not. He held the cup as if it were a jewel, with exaggerated solicitude. I drank the coffee. I kept waiting for him to leave. He didn't leave. He asked me what I wanted to eat. And then I remembered that my friend hadn't come, and I realized it was she who had sent him. And my rage was directed at her, at all those who think they can help you with the laws of the ant heap, their arbitrary concept of right and wrong. Jesus, Mary, and Joseph. Why Joseph? Mary's doing well with only her baby. The only thing acceptable in the whole legend is just this rapport between the two of them: the marvelous lie about an egg that gets filled by parthenogenesis. Why is Joseph there all of a sudden? What good is he? To lead the donkey that's too stubborn to move? To cut the umbilical cord and make sure the whole placenta has emerged? Or else to save the reputation of an irresponsible girl who got pregnant without having a husband? Unless he's just following after her like a servant so that she'll forgive him for having asked her to have an abortion. I watched him kneeling on the floor to gather up the scattered petals and couldn't feel the slightest friendship toward him. By coming here he'd thrown everything off balance. He'd broken a symmetry, disturbed a complicity: the one that existed between you and me. A stranger had arrived, you see, and placed himself between us, and it was as though someone had brought a piece of furniture that isn't needed, that clutters the room, shuts out light, takes up space, and gets in the way. Maybe if he'd been with us from the beginning, his presence now would have seemed normal and even necessary: we wouldn't have been able to conceive of any other way of preparing for your arrival. But to see him descend like this—out of nowhere, with the inappropriateness of the intruder who joins two people when they want to be alone, the indiscretion of someone who sits down at your table though you've neither invited nor encouraged him—was almost offensive. I would have liked to say, "Please go away. We have no need of you, nor Joseph, nor God Almighty. We don't need a father, we don't need a husband, you're one too many." But I couldn't. Maybe I was held back because I am timid, a person who doesn't know how to get rid of someone who sits down at her table without asking permission. Maybe I was held back by a sense of pity that little by little became understanding, regret. Beyond his weakness, his cowardice, who can say how much he had really suffered, he too? Who can say how much it had cost him to keep silent, to force himself to come here with a lousy bunch of flowers? No one is born by parthenogenesis; the drop of light that had pierced the egg was his, half of the nucleus that had started your body on its way was his. And the fact that I had forgotten it was the price we were paying for the only law that no one acknowledges: a man and a woman meet, they like each other, desire each other, perhaps love each other, and after a while they no longer love each other, no longer desire each other, no longer like each other, and may even wish they'd never met. I've found what I was looking for, Child: what people call love between a man and a woman is a season. And if, at its flowering, this season is a feast of greenery, at its waning, it's only a heap of rotting leaves.

I let him fix supper. I let him open that absurd bottle of

champagne. (Where had he hidden it when he came in?) I let him take a bath. (He kept whistling in the bathroom as though everything had been settled.) And I allowed him to sleep here, in our bed. But this morning, as soon as he left, I felt a kind of shame. And now I feel as though I've failed in some duty, as though I've betrayed you. Let's hope he never comes back.

* * *

To WALK IN THE STREET after all those days in bed! To feel the wind on your face, the sun in your eyes, to see other people, to look at life! If the doctor's office hadn't been so far, I would have gone on foot, singing. I hailed a taxi instead. The driver was a bastard. He was smoking a big fat cigar that nauseated me; he jolted me around by needlessly applying his brakes. We had hardly started when I felt a cramp, and my joy evaporated in the usual nervousness. In the doctor's office there was a row of women with swollen bellies. When the receptionist asked me to wait, I became irritated. I didn't care to take my place in line with a lot of women with swollen bellies. I had nothing in common with them. Not even the belly. Mine isn't swollen, you can hardly tell. Finally I went in, undressed, and lay down on the table. The doctor tortured you with his finger, pressing and probing, then he took off his rubber glove and asked in an icy voice: "Do you really want this child?" I couldn't believe my ears. "Of course. Why?" I answered. "Because many women say they want it but subconsciously they don't want it at all. Even without realizing it, they do everything to keep it from being born." I was indignant. I wasn't there to have my good faith put on trial nor even to discuss psychoanalysis, I said; I was there to find out how you were doing. His tone changed and politely he explained what he meant. There were things he didn't understand in this pregnancy. He thought the egg seemed well placed, in a normal position. He thought the growth of the fetus was proceeding well, in a regular manner. And yet something was wrong. The uterus, for instance, was too sensitive, it contracted much too easily, and this gave rise to the suspicion that blood wasn't flowing properly to the placenta. Had I stayed immobile as he had ordered? I answered yes. Had I abstained from alcohol and cut down on smoking, as he'd recommended? I answered yes. Had I perhaps exerted myself too much, become fatigued? I answered no. Had I had sexual relations? Again I answered no. And it was true: I hadn't let your father get close to me the other night, though he had kept repeating how cruel I was. Then the doctor looked perplexed: "Are you worried about anything?" I answered yes. "Have you had some kind of psychological shock, any trouble?" I hesitated this time before answering yes, and he stared at me without asking what kind of shock, what kind of trouble. Then he explained. Sometimes worries, anxieties, shocks are more dangerous than physical fatigue, since they lead to cramps, uterine contractions, and seriously threaten the life of the embryo. One mustn't forget that the uterus is connected with the pituitary gland, that any stimulus is immediately transmitted to the genital organs: a violent surprise, pain, rage can provoke a partial detachment of the egg. Even constant nervousness, a perpetual state of anxiety, can do it. One could speak, and far be it from him to overstep the boundaries into science fiction or parapsychology, of a thought that kills. At the unconscious level, of course. For this reason, he said, he absolutely insisted that I stay quiet. I must strictly avoid all emotion, all dark moods. Serenity, placidity were the watchwords.

"Doctor," I answered, "you might as well ask me to change the color of my eyes: how can I be placid if it's not my nature to be so?" Coldly he looked me up and down again. "That's your business. You'll have to manage it. Put on some weight." Then he prescribed some pills against cramps, as well as other medication. If by chance a drop of blood appeared, I was to run to him.

I'm frightened. And also angry at you. What do you think I am: a container, a jar where you put some object for safekeeping? I'm a woman, for God's sake, I'm a person. I can't unscrew my head and keep myself from thinking. I can't erase my emotions or keep myself from showing them. I can't ignore a feeling of rage, or joy, or sorrow. I have my own reactions, sometimes astonishment, sometimes dismay. Even if I could suppress myself, I wouldn't want to be reduced to the state of a vegetable or a physiological machine good for nothing but procreation! What a lot of demands you make, Child. First you lay claim to my body and deprive it of its most elementary right: to move around. Then you even pretend to control my heart and mind, atrophying them, blocking them, robbing them of their capacity to feel, think, live! You even accuse my unconscious. That's too much, I can't accept it. If we're to stay together, Child, we'd better come to terms. I'll make you a concession: I'll put on weight, I'll give you my body, but my mind, no. My reactions, no. Those I keep for myself. And along with them I claim the reward of my own little pleasures. In fact, I'm now drinking a good slug of whisky and smoking a pack of cigarettes, one after another, and getting back to my work, my existence as a person and not as a container, and crying, crying, crying: without asking you if it hurts. Because I'm fed up with you!

* * *

FORGIVE ME. I must have been drunk, out of my mind. Look at all these cigarette butts, and look at this wet handkerchief. What a crisis of imbecile fury, what a disgusting scene. Pure selfishness. How are you, Child? Better than I am, I hope. I'm exhausted. I'm so tired that I'd like to hold out for another six months, just the time needed to give birth to you, and then die. You'd take my place in the world and I'd rest. Nor would it be too soon: it seems to me that by now I've seen everything there was to see. And once you're out of my body, you won't need me any more. Any woman capable of loving you will be an excellent mother for you: the call of the blood doesn't exist, it's an invention. The mother isn't the one who carries you in her womb, she's the woman who raises you. Or the man who raises you. I could give you to your father. He came back a while ago and brought me a blue rose. He said blue is the color for a boy. Obviously he wants you to be a boy: that would be more to his credit, a sign of superiority. Poor man. It's not his fault; he too has been told that God is an old man with a white beard, that Mary was an incubator, that without Joseph she wouldn't even have found a stable, that the one to bring fire was Prometheus. I don't despise him for this. But I still say that neither you nor I has any need for him. Nor for his blue rose. I told him to go away, to leave us alone. He swayed as though I'd hit him with a stick, started toward the door, went away without answering. We're about to go out ourselves: to work. The boss has given me his assurances again, adding, however, that commitments have to be respected: a pregnant woman can leave her job only in the sixth month. He's also reminded me of the trip, along with a politely veiled threat to shift the assignment to a man because certain-accidents-don't-happen-to-a-man. It was all I could do to keep from hitting him, and I started prevaricating. The next ten days will be tough; I must make up for lost time. But I'll tell you one thing: the thought of going back to work shakes me out of this torpor, this resignation that makes me dream of death. Thank God winter has begun: people won't notice my swollen stomach under my overcoat. And from now on it's going to keep swelling. This morning it's more swollen and my dress is too tight. At fourteen weeks, do you know how long you are? At least four inches. Even the placenta, still too small to envelop the amniotic sac, is drawing aside. And you're invading me without pity.

* * *

I'M NOT ONE TO BE frightened at the sight of blood. To be a woman is a schooling in blood: every month we pay an odious homage to it. But when I saw that tiny spot on the pillow, my eyes clouded and my legs shook. I fell into panic, then despair, and I cursed myself. I accused myself of every sort of negligence toward you, you who couldn't protect yourself, couldn't rebel, so small and defenseless and at the mercy of all my caprices and irresponsibility. It wasn't even red, that spot. It was pink, a light pink. Nevertheless it was more than enough to transmit your message, to announce that perhaps you were dying. I seized the pillow and ran. The doctor was unexpectedly kind. He received me even though it was evening and told me to calm myself: you weren't dying, you hadn't broken loose, you had only suffered. It was only a threatening signal. Absolute rest would take care of everything, so long as it was absolute, so long as I didn't get out of bed even to go to the bathroom, and for this reason it would be better if I went to the hospital. We're in the hospital. A sad room in this sad world. We've been here a week, a week I've spent practically always asleep, numbed by sedatives. Now they've suspended them, but it's worse: I don't know how to pass the time, which hangs so heavily. I've asked for the newspapers and they don't bring them. I've asked for a television set and they won't give it to me. I've asked for a telephone, but it doesn't work. No sign of my friend. Nor even your father. I feel crushed and brutalized by the silence. I'm a prisoner of a female beast dressed in white who comes around every so often with a shot of lutein and scornfully injects me; I don't succeed even in trying to transmit a little tenderness to you. But long-slumbering reflections, stifled in vain, rise to the surface of my mind to cry out things that I didn't know I knew. Why should I have to bear this agony? In the name of what? Of a crime committed by embracing a man? Of a cell split into two cells and then into four cells and then into eight, ad infinitum, without my wanting it, without my asking? Or else in the name of life? All right, life. But what is this life by which you, who exist still incomplete, count for more than I, who exist complete already? What is this respect for you that removes respect for me? What is this right of yours to exist that takes no account of my right to exist? There's no humanity in you. Humanity! Are you a human being, you? Are a little bubble of an egg and a sperm of five microns really enough to make a human being? The human being is myself, who can think and speak and laugh and cry and act in a world that acts to build ideas and things. You're nothing but a little flesh doll that can't think, can't speak, can't laugh, can't cry, and can act only to build itself. What I see in you isn't you: it's myself! I've bestowed a mind on you, carried on a dialogue with you, but your mind was my mind, and our dialogue a monologue: mine! Enough of this comedy, this delirium. No one is human by natural right, before being born. We become human afterward, when we're born, because we stay with others, because others help us, because a mother or a woman or a man or somebody teaches us to eat, to walk, to speak, to think, to behave like humans. The only thing that joins us, my dear, is an umbilical cord. And we're not a couple. We're persecutor and persecuted. You the persecutor and I the persecuted. You wormed your way into me like a thief, and you carried away my womb, my blood, my breath. Now you'd like to steal my whole existence. I won't let you. And since I've arrived at the point of telling you these sacred truths, do you know what I conclude? I don't see why I should have a child. I've never felt at ease with children. I've never been able to deal with them. When I approach them with a smile, they scream as though I'd hit them. The job of a mother doesn't suit me. I have other duties in life. I have a job that I like and I intend to go on with it. I have a future awaiting me and I don't intend to abandon it. Those who absolve an impoverished woman who doesn't want more children, who absolve a girl who's been raped and doesn't want that child, had better absolve me too. To be poor, to be raped, doesn't constitute the only justification. I'm going to leave this hospital and take that assignment. Then let come what may. If you succeed in being born, you'll be born. If you don't succeed, you'll die. I'm not going to kill you, understand: I simply refuse to help you to exercise your tyranny to the end, and . . .

This wasn't our pact, I realize. But a pact is an agreement wherein one gives to receive, and how could I know when we signed it that you'd claim everything and give me nothing? Besides you didn't sign it at all, I was the only one to sign. That alters its validity. You didn't sign it and I've never had any message of assent from you: your only message has been a pink drop of blood. I shall be cursed forever and my life shall become a perpetual lament beyond death itself, but I shall not change my decision.

* * *

HE CALLED ME A MURDERESS. Encased in his white jacket, no longer a doctor but a judge, he thundered that I was failing in the most fundamental duties of a mother, a woman, a citizen. He shouted that even to leave the hospital would be a crime, to get out of bed a serious act, but to undertake a trip is premeditated homicide and the law should punish me as it punishes any murderer. Then he began to beseech me, trying to persuade me with your photograph. Just take a good look, if I had any heart at all: you were now a child in all respects. Your mouth was no longer the notion of a mouth: it was a mouth. Your nose was no longer the notion of a nose: it was a nose. Your face was no longer the sketch of a face: it was a face. And the same for your body, your hands, your feet where even the toenails could be seen. You also have the beginning of hair on your well-formed little head. And I should realize your fragility, he continued. Look at your skin: so delicate, so diaphanous, that every vein, every capillary, every nerve could be seen through it. Nor were you tiny any more: you measured at least six and a quarter inches and weighed seven ounces. If I wanted to have an abortion, I wouldn't be able to: it was now too late. And yet I was setting out to do something worse than an abortion, he said. I listened without batting an eyelash. Then I signed a paper wherein he declined any responsibility for your life and mine, and I assumed it in his stead. I watched him leave the room in the grip of a fury that made him blue in the face. And just at that moment, you moved. You did what I had waited for, yearned for, for months. You stretched yourself, perhaps yawned, and gave me a little blow. A little kick. Your first kick . . . like the kick I gave my mother to tell her not to throw me away. My legs turned to marble. And for several seconds I sat there breathless, my temples throbbing. I also felt a burning in my throat, a tear that blinded my eyes. Then the tear rolled down and fell on the sheet, making a little plop. But I got out of bed all the same. I packed my suitcase all the same. Tomorrow we leave. By plane.

* * *

WAS IT REALLY NECESSARY to get so upset? We're doing fine in the country we've come to. We did fine during the whole trip and after arrival. Never a cramp, a pain, or any nausea. Nothing that the doctor foresaw has happened: this was confirmed by the woman doctor who examined me yesterday. Nice woman. Having palpated you, she's concluded that she sees no reason for alarm; her colleague went too far in his caution and pessimism. What's a little drop of blood? There are women who lose blood for the entire period of their pregnancy and still give birth to healthy children. In her opinion, staying in bed is against nature and also carrying precaution too far. For instance, one of her patients, a professional ballerina, had gone on performing the pas de deux until after the fifth month.

The only thing that surprised her about me was the fact that my womb is hardly swollen, but the ballerina too had a nearly flat stomach. I could even continue the medication prescribed by her colleague if I cared to, but above all I was to let nature take its course. Her only warning was not to drive the car too much. I told her I'd have to make a trip by car of at least ten days. She raised her eyebrows, somewhat bewildered, and asked if it was really necessary. I answered yes. She was silent a moment and then said never mind, the roads in this country are comfortable and smooth, the cars in this country have good springs. The important thing is not to overdo it and to allow myself a rest every two or three hours. Are you listening? I'm saying that I've made peace with you, that we're friends at last! I'm saying that I'm sorry to have distrusted and mistreated you and that I'm sorrier still if you stay offended and stop giving me little kicks. You haven't given me any, since the hospital. Sometimes when I think of it, I frown.

But that doesn't last long, and soon I'm calm again. Have you any idea how much I've changed? Since going back to my regular life, I feel like a new person: a seagull in flight. Was there really a moment when I wanted to die? Insane. Life is so beautiful, and so is light. And the trees are beautiful, and the earth and the sea. There's a lot of sea here: does its perfume reach you, its roar? Also it's beautiful to work if joy is quivering inside you. I was lying when I told you that work is forever tiring and humiliating. You must forgive me: rage and anxiety made me see only darkness. And speaking of darkness, my impatience to bring you forth has come over me again. And with it, the fear of having discouraged you with all my talk about freedom that doesn't exist, about solitude's being the only possible condition. Forget that foolishness: it's good to be side by side. Life is a community in which we hold hands, to help and console each other. Even plants bloom better alongside each other, birds migrate in flocks, and fish swim in shoals. What would we do by ourselves? We'd feel like astronauts on the moon, stifled by fear and our impatience to go back to earth. Hurry up, Child, get these remaining months over with, lean forth with no fear of watching the sun. At first it will dazzle you, frighten you, but soon it will become such gaiety that you won't be able to do without it. I regret having always given you the most ugly examples and never having told you about the splendor of a dawn, the sweetness of a kiss, the aroma of a meal. I regret never having made you laugh. Were you to judge me by the fairy tales I told you, you'd have every right to conclude that I'm a sort of Electra eternally dressed in black. From now on you must imagine me a Peter Pan, dressed in yellow and green and red, and ready to spread garlands of flowers on the roofs and the bell towers and on the clouds so they won't turn into rain. We'll be happy together because deep inside I'm a child myself. Would you believe that I like to play? Last night when I came back to the hotel, I mixed up all the shoes that had been placed outside the rooms, and the breakfast orders too. You should have heard the uproar this morning. One lady found a pair of men's loafers and demanded her high-heeled sandals, a man found a pair of sneakers and wanted his boots, someone protested that they'd brought him only coffee when he'd ordered ham and eggs, and another complained that he didn't want a Christmas dinner, only tea with lemon. My ear to the door, I listened and laughed, so amused that I felt as though I'd returned to my childhood, to the time when I was happy because every gesture was a game.

* * *

I'VE BOUGHT YOU A CRADLE. Then, when I had bought it, it occurred to me that, according to some, owning a cradle before the child is born brings bad luck, like flowers on the bed. But superstitions don't bother me any more. It's an Indian cradle, the kind you carry like a knapsack on the back. It's yellow and green and red like Peter Pan. I'll load you on my back, I'll carry you everywhere, and people will smile and say: Look at those two crazy kids. I've also bought you a wardrobe: little shirts, overalls, and a beautiful carillon. It plays a merry waltz. When I told my friend about it on the telephone, she commented that I'm completely out of my mind. But her voice was happy, freed of the anxiety that gripped her the day we left: And-what-if-you-lose-it-on-the-plane? She who in the beginning advised me to get rid of you! She's really a good woman. In fact, I've never been able to reproach her for the day she sent your father. And as for him, any man understanding enough to put up with me the night I kicked him out is not a man to be discarded. Later he wrote me a letter, and I was moved. I'm a coward, he admitted, because I am a man; yet I must be absolved because I am a man. An atavistic instinct, I suppose, drives him to want you. We'll see what to do with him: sometimes a piece of furniture we don't need turns out to be useful, and certainly I have no desire to be his enemy. Everyone is included in this truce with the ant heap: your father, the doctors, the boss. If you'd only seen my boss when I announced our departure. He kept saying, "Now that's good news! Good girl, you won't regret it!"

I won't regret it. It's only by respecting herself that a woman can demand respect from others. It's only by believing in herself that she can be believed in by others. Good-night, Child, tomorrow we start our trip by car. I'd like to write you a poem that would tell of my relief, my rediscovered faith, this wish to spread garlands of flowers on the roofs, the bell towers, the clouds, this sensation of flying like a seagull in the blue, far from all the filth and melancholy, over a sea that always looks clean from on high. Actually courage is optimism. I wasn't optimistic because I wasn't courageous.

* * *

THE ROADS OF THIS COUNTRY are comfortable and smooth, the cars in this country have good springs: lady doctor, you too lie. And I am not a seagull. Now what do I do, Child? Shall I keep going? Shall I go back? If I go back, it's worse: I'll have to go over the same impossible route. If instead I go forward, there's hope it may improve. Had I the courage of rhetoric, I could say I'm driving along a road that's just like my life: all holes and stones and snags. I once knew a writer who liked to say that everybody gets the kind of life he deserves. Like saying a poor man deserves to be poor, a blind man deserves to be blind. He was a stupid man, though he was an intelligent writer. The thread that divides intelligence from stupidity is very thin, as you'll find out. Once it breaks, the two things merge together like love and hate, life and death, whether you're a man or a woman. I keep wondering whether you will be a man or a woman, and now I'd like you to be a man. So you wouldn't have the monthly lesson of blood, and you wouldn't feel guilty one day for driving along a road full of holes and stones. You wouldn't suffer as I do at this moment and you could free yourself to fly in the blue much more seriously than I can. My efforts to fly never go beyond the flutter of a turkey. Perhaps the women who burn their bras are right. Or are they? Not one of them has discovered a system whereby the world wouldn't end if they didn't give birth to their children. And children are born of women. I know a science-fiction story that takes place on a planet where in order to procreate you must belong to a group of seven people. But it's very difficult to get seven people together, and still more difficult for them to come to an agreement, because not only conception but pregnancy as well involves all seven. Therefore the race becomes extinct and the planet empty. There is another story in which all the hero needs is an alkaline solution, a glass of water with salt. He jumps into it and bang! He becomes two. It's just a normal cellular division, and at the moment the hero splits, he ceases to be himself: he commits a kind of suicide of his ego. But he doesn't die and doesn't suffer nine months of hell. Of hell? For some women, they're nine months of glory. The best way is still what I told you in the beginning. You take the embryo from the mother's womb and put it in the womb of another woman who's ready to shelter it, a mother more patient than I, more generous than I . . . I think I'm getting a fever. The cramps have started again. I must ignore them. But how? By thinking about other things, I guess. I could tell you a fairy tale. I haven't told you one in a long time.

Once upon a time there was a woman who dreamed of a little piece of moon. Although a little bit of dust would have been enough for her. It wasn't an impossible dream, not even bizarre. She knew the men who went to the moon, for at that time it was the fashion to go there. The men departed from a point on the earth not too far from here, in little iron ships hooked to the top of a very high rocket, and every time the rocket shot into the sky, roaring and scattering flowers of fire like a comet, the woman was happy. She cried to the rocket: "Go, go, go!" Then anxiously and jealously she followed the voyage of the men who flew for three days and three nights in the darkness. The men who went to the moon were stupid men. They had stupid faces of stone and they didn't know how to laugh, they didn't know how to cry. For them going to the moon was a scientific feat and nothing else, an achievement of technology. During the trip they never said anything poetic, only numbers and formulas and boring information; when they showed a bit of humanity it was only to ask for the latest football scores. Once they landed on the moon, they had even less to say. At most they uttered two or three prepared statements, then they planted a tin flag, and with robot-like movements they performed a ceremony of mundane gestures. They departed for earth, having fouled the moon with their excrements, which thus remained to testify to the passage of Man. The excrements were enclosed in boxes, the boxes were left there with the flag, and, if you knew it, you were never able to look at the moon again without saying: "Their excrements are up there, too." Finally they came back, with a load of rocks and dust. Moon rocks, moon dust—the dust that the woman was dreaming of. And when she saw them again, she begged (I begged): "Will you give me a little moon? You have so much of it!" But they always answered: We-cannot-it-is-forbidden. All their moon ended up in the laboratories, on the desks of the people for whom going there was a scientific feat and nothing else, an achievement of technology. They were stupid men, because they were men without soul. And yet there was one who seemed to me a little better. Because he knew how to laugh and cry. He was an ugly little man with gaps between his teeth and a great fear in his heart. To conceal his fear, he laughed and wore ridiculous hats that gave him something like a soul, you see. This was why I was a friend of his, and because he knew he didn't deserve the moon. Each time we met, he grumbled, "What shall I say up there? I'm not a poet, I don't know how to say profound and beautiful things." A few days before going to the moon, he came to say good-bye to me and ask me what to say on the moon. I told him he should say something true, something honest—for instance, that he was a little man brimming with fear because he was a little man. He liked that and swore, "If I come back, I'll bring you a little moon. Moon dust." He left and came back. But he came back changed. If I telephoned him to remind him of his promise, he answered evasively. Then one night he invited me to dinner at his home and I rushed there thinking he was finally going to give me some moon. I was restless at the table; the dinner seemed endless. Finally, he said, "Now I'll show you the moon." He didn't say, "Now I'll give you the moon," but I didn't notice the difference. He still wore those ridiculous hats, he still laughed those ridiculous laughs. I didn't suspect that while in the sky, he had lost even the drop of soul I had attributed to him.

Winking, he took me into his office and opened a locked closet. Inside were a number of objects: a kind of spade, a hoe, a tube, all covered with a strange silver-gray dust. Moon dust. My heart began to beat wildly. I reached out a hand and gently grasped the spade, which was light, almost weightless. The dust on it was like face powder, a veil of silver that remained on the skin like a second skin. It is difficult to describe what I felt at seeing the moon on my skin. Perhaps it was the sensation of expanding in time and space or, by reaching the unreachable, the very idea of the infinite. This is what I think now—at that moment I could not think. Even now, as I scrupulously search my mind, I can only tell you that I stood there dazed, holding the spade in my hand; and I wasn't aware that he was becoming impatient. When I realized it, I gave the spade back to him and murmured, "Thanks. Now may I have the dust?" He immediately turned cold. "What dust?" "The moon dust you promised me." He answered, "You had it. I let you touch it." I thought he was joking. It took minutes that seemed longer than years for me to realize he wasn't joking, that he thought he had fulfilled his promise by the act of letting me touch the spade. This is what you do with the poor when you let them admire a jewel in a shop window or watch a feast from afar where they're not allowed to participate. In my surprise, my sorrow, I wasn't even able to throw it back in his face, to reproach him for his meanness. I only thought: how could I convince him that this is too cruel? And in this hope I began to beg him, explaining that I wasn't asking for a piece of moon, all I was asking for was the moon dust he had promised me, only a pinch, he had so much in the closet, every object was covered with it, all he had to do was let me collect a little of it on a sheet of paper, on something that wasn't my skin, so that I could look at it again and again in the years to come. It had always been a dream of mine; he knew it wasn't a whim. But the more I groveled, the more hostile he became, staring at me coldly, without speaking. Finally, in silence, he locked the closet and left the room. From the living room his wife asked if we wanted coffee.

I didn't answer. I stood there looking at my hand covered with the moon. I had the moon in my hand, and I didn't know where to lay it down, how to keep it. At the slightest contact it would disappear. Vainly my brain sought a solution, some way of saving what might be saved, but all I found was a fog, and inside the fog a sentence: "It would be like removing face powder. Wherever I smear it, it's lost." And this was the greatest torment, a torture that Tantalus had never known. Tantalus saw the fruit disappear the moment he was about to grasp it; he didn't see it disappear once having grasped it. So I gave a last look at my silvery hand, still open in a gesture of absurd supplication, swallowed my wish to cry, and smiled bitterly. Over infinite distances the moon had come to me and alighted on my skin, and now I was about to throw it away. Forever. Even if I had wanted to, I wouldn't have been able to stay like this, with my fingers outstretched, and without touching other things. Sooner or later I would have put my fingers on something, you understand; everything would vanish like smoke in the air. And all for the cruel joke of a cruel imbecile. I clenched my fist with anger. I opened it again. Now all I could see on the palm was a faint arabesque of dirty, twisted lines, disgusting to look at. Had I dreamed and waited so long only to arrive at disgust? I wiped my palm on the closet door. It left an oily print, like the slime of a snail, like the trace of a long tear.

When I left the house, the moon was shining and illuminating the night with its whiteness. I gazed at it with misted eyes and thought: as soon as something white and clean exists, there's always someone to soil it with his excrements. Then I wondered: Why? But why? In the hotel I opened the faucet and put my hand under it. A dark liquid drained away and soon disappeared in a dark whirlpool. Child, you're like my moon, my moon dust. The cramps have increased, I can't drive any more. If only I can find a motel, someplace to stop and rest. Maybe when my mind is clearer, I'll find a way of saving what can be saved: of not throwing away my moon. I don't want to lose the moon again, to see it vanish again at the bottom of a washbasin. But it's hopeless. With the same certainty that paralyzed me the night I knew you existed, I now know that you're dying.

* * *

I INTERRUPTED MY TRIP, went back to the city, and phoned the doctor. She didn't believe it. She kept telling me to keep calm; two weeks ago everything was going well; it was surely my imagination. I answered that blood is not imagination, that for a week I'd been holed up in a motel, and the only result had been blood. I went to see her right away. At the door she smiled, with her usual optimism. I undressed quickly, before she had a chance to speak. I lay down on the table and she put her hand on my heart. "How your heart is beating! It's as loud as a drum." I didn't respond either to her kindness or her smile. The sympathy of others was no good to me now. I felt the certainty of participating in a needless ceremony, one secretly expected and perhaps desired. I was ready, resigned, convinced I would not react, since everything there was to say had already been said, everything there was to suffer had already been suffered. But when the ceremony began, I understood that I would never be ready. Even listening to her questions hurt me, even answering them. "Haven't you felt it move recently?" "No." "Have you felt heavier, more awkward, these past days?" "No." "And when did you get the idea that . . . ?" "On that bumpy road, before getting to the motel." "That's not enough to go by. And it's up to me to decide, isn't it?" Then she uncovered my stomach, noting that actually it looked flatter than before. She palpated my breasts, observing that actually they seemed less swollen than before. She put on the rubber glove, she tried to feel you. And her forehead wrinkled, her eyes darkened, as she said, "The uterus has lost its resiliency. It seems shrunken. There's a possibility that the child is not growing properly or not growing any more. We'll have to make a biological examination to make sure; wait another few days." Then she took off the glove and threw it aside. She leaned forward with both hands on the table. She gazed at me sadly. "No, I might as well tell you at once. You're right. It's stopped growing—at least two weeks ago and perhaps three. Try to be brave. It's over. It's dead."

I gave no answer. I made no sign. I didn't even blink. I lay there with a body that was all stone and silence. My brain too was stone and silence. Not a thought, not a word, could take root. The only sensation was an unbearable weight on the stomach, an invisible leaden weight as crushing as though the sky had fallen on me without making any sound. In this absolute immobility, this absolute lack of sound, her words exploded like a roar of gunshot: "Come on, get up. Get dressed." I got up and my legs were stone within stone. I had to make an inhuman effort to make them obey. I got dressed and heard my own voice asking what I would have to do. "Nothing. It will stay there for a while. Then it will go spontaneously." I nodded. Then her distant voice started piling sentence on sentence, an incessant droning that urged me not to be disheartened, many children are lost because they're not perfect, not properly formed, no one likes to bring a child into the world who's not perfect, not properly formed. I shouldn't condemn myself, I shouldn't reproach myself for things I wasn't guilty of, pregnancy is like that when it's allowed to develop naturally, she was opposed to the system that confines a woman to bed for months and keeps nature from taking its course. I paid the bill. I said good-bye to her with a nod of my head. I went out between two rows of swollen bellies, which seemed to accuse my flat stomach that enclosed a corpse. Finally I thought: What has happened is as it was meant to be; I must stay coherent. And the word *coherent* accompanied me to the hotel, hammering obsessively: coherent, coherent, coherent. But when I entered my room and saw the cradle, saw the carillon, saw the little shirts of your wardrobe, a moan escaped me. And I fell on the bed, while another moan followed the first, then another, and still another, until from the depths of my body, where you lie like a little useless piece of meat, there emerged a great cry, which cracked the stone, breaking it into a thousand pieces, crumbling it to dust. I screamed—and fainted.

* * *

Perhaps it was while I slept, or perhaps it was during the delirium . . . Anyway it happened, and I remember it clearly. There was a spotless white room, with seven benches and a cage. I was inside the cage and they were on the benches, distant and unreachable. On the central bench sat the male doctor who had taken care of me before my trip. To his right sat the woman doctor, to his left my boss. Next to my boss was my friend and next to her your father. Next to the woman doctor sat my parents. No one else. And there were no objects anywhere, on neither walls nor floor. But I immediately understood that a trial was taking place in which I was the accused and that these people were the jury. I felt neither panic nor dismay. With infinite resignation, I began to study them, one by one. Your father sobbed softly, covering his face as on the day he came to visit me. My parents kept their heads bowed, almost as though weighed down by a deadly weariness or a deadly sorrow. My friend seemed sad, the three others unfathomable. The doctor got up and began reading a sheet of paper: "The defendant being present, this jury has come together to judge her for the crime of premeditated homicide in having desired and provoked the death of her child through indifference, selfishness, a lack of the most elementary respect for its right to life." Then he put down the paper and explained how the trial would be conducted. Each was to speak as witness and judge, then state aloud his or her vote: guilty or not guilty. The majority votes would determine the verdict and, in case of conviction, choose the penalty. So now the trial could begin. It was up to him to speak first. His words rose like an icy wind.

"A child is not a decayed tooth. One cannot simply extract it and throw it in the garbage along with the dirty cotton and gauze. A child is a person, and the life of a person is a continuum from the moment it is conceived to the moment it dies. Some of you will contest the very concept of the continuum. You will say that at the moment of conception, one does not exist as a person. We exist only as a cell that can multiply but not represent life. Or no more, say, than it is represented by a tree that it's no crime to cut down, a gnat that it's no crime to crush. As a scientist, let me say at once that a tree does not become a man, and neither does a gnat. All the elements that go to make up a man, from his body to his personality, all the quotients that constitute an individual, from his blood to his mind, are concentrated in that cell. They represent much more than a plan or a promise. If we were able to examine them with a microscope capable of seeing beyond the visible, we would go down on our knees and all believe in God. Therefore, paradoxical as it may seem, I feel entitled to use the word murder. And let me add: if humanity depended on volume, murder on quantity, we would have to conclude that to kill a man weighing two hundred pounds is more serious than to kill one weighing a hundred. I ask the colleague sitting to my right not to look so amused. On her arguments I reserve judgment, but on her way of exercising the medical profession I do not reserve comment: in that cage there should be not one woman, but two." He looked at the woman doctor with scorn and severity. Smoking a cigarette, she calmly met his gaze, and that consoled me and brought me a little warmth. But the icy voice resumed at once.

"Nevertheless we are not here to judge the death of a cell. We are here to judge the death of a child who had attained at least three months of its prenatal existence. Who or what provoked its death? Natural circumstances unknown to us? Someone who has gone scot-free? Or the woman you see there in the cage? I can prove to you that it was the woman you see in the cage who provoked its death. Not by chance did I suspect her from the beginning. I have had enough experience to recognize infanticide, even behind the mask she wore when she said that she wanted the child. It was a lie addressed to herself before being addressed to others. I was struck, for instance, by her hardness, like steel. The day I congratulated her on the positive results of her test, she answered curtly that she already knew. I was also struck by her reactions of hostility when ordered to stay in bed after experiencing cramps due to uterine contraction. She couldn't afford the luxury, she answered, and two weeks was the most time she would allow. I had to insist, to get angry, to plead with her to accept my recommendations. And this convinced me that she had no wish to accept the duties of a mother, that her maternal state was not a responsible one. Moreover, she phoned me repeatedly to say she was well and that there was no reason to keep her in bed, protesting that she had a job and had to get up. The morning I saw her again she was the picture of unhappiness. And it was during that examination that my suspicions became stronger, and I saw that this woman was contemplating a crime. There was no anatomical or physiological reason why her pregnancy should be so painful: the cramps could only have a psychological, that is to say deliberate, origin. I questioned her. She admitted, laconically, that she had a number of anxieties. She also alluded to some sorrow, which I made no effort to uncover, since it seemed obvious that her sorrow lay in being pregnant. Finally I asked her if she really wanted the child, explaining to her that sometimes thoughts can kill: she would have to convert her anxiety into placidity.

She flared up angrily and said it would be like asking her to change the color of her eyes. A few days later she came back. She had resumed her normal life and matters had worsened. I put her in the hospital, where I kept her immobilized for a week and was able to keep her psyche under control by the use of drugs.

"And now we come to the crime, ladies and gentlemen. But before I go into that, let me say: Suppose that one of you is gravely ill and needs a particular medicine. The medicine is within reach. Salvation consists in the simple gesture of someone's handing it to you. What do you call someone who, instead of giving you the medicine, pours it out and replaces it with a poison? Insane? Malicious? Guilty of withholding assistance? No, that's not enough. I call him a murderer. Ladies and gentlemen of the jury, there is no doubt that the child was ill and that the medicine within reach was immobility. But this woman not only withheld its use, she administered the poison of a journey that would have damaged even an easier pregnancy. Hours and hours by airplane, by car, along bumpy, disconnected roads, all by herself. I implored her. I explained to her that at that point her child was no longer a proliferation of cells but an actual baby. I warned her she would kill it. She objected with unrelenting harshness. She signed a paper whereby she assumed all responsibility. She left. She killed it. Of course, if we were before a court of written laws, I would be hard put to maintain her guilt. There were no probes or drugs or surgical incisions. According to written law, this woman would have to be absolved, since that fact does not exist. But we are a jury of life, ladies and gentlemen, and in the name of life

I tell you that her behavior was worse than probes and drugs and surgical incisions. Because she was hypocritical, cowardly, and ran no legal risks.

"I should be very glad to recognize extenuating circumstances and partly absolve her. But I see neither where nor how. Was she, perhaps, poor, floundering in economic circumstances that made her unable to support a child? Absolutely not. She recognizes that herself. Did she have to defend her honor because society would have persecuted her had she brought an illegitimate child into the world? Not even that. She belongs to a cultural establishment that not only would not have rejected her but would have made a heroine of her; and, in any case, she does not believe in the rules of society. She rejects God, her country, the family, marriage, the very principles of living together in society. Her crime has no extenuating aspects because she committed it in the name of a certain freedom: a personal, selfish freedom that takes no account of others and their rights. I have used the word *rights.* I have done so to forestall the word *euthanasia.* I've also done so to keep you from replying that, by letting this child die, she was exercising her right: the right to spare the community the burden of a sick and thus faulty individual. It is not for us to decide *a priori* who is to be faulty and who not. Homer was blind and Leopardi a hunchback. Had the Spartans thrown them from the rocks, had their mothers wearied of carrying them in their wombs, humanity today would be all the poorer. I refuse to accept that an Olympic champion is worth more than a crippled poet. As for the sacrifice of guarding the fetus of an Olympic champion or a crippled poet in the womb, let me remind you that, whether we like it or not, that is the way the human race is propagated. And my verdict is Guilty!"

I went numb at that shout. I closed my eyes, so I didn't see the woman doctor as she got up to speak. When I looked up, she had already begun:

"My colleague has forgotten to add that for every Homer a Hitler is born, that every conception is a challenge replete with splendid and horrible possibilities. I don't know whether this child would have been a Joan of Arc or a Hitler: when it died, it was only an unknown possibility. But I do know who this woman is: a reality that must not be destroyed. Between an unknown possibility and a reality that must not be destroyed, I choose the latter. My colleague seems obsessed by the cult of life. But he reserves that cult for those to come. He does not extend it to those who are already here. The cult of life is nothing but rhetoric. Even the remark a-child-is-not-a-decayed-tooth is nothing but a clever remark. I'm sure my colleague has been in the war and fired his gun and killed, forgetting all the while that neither at the age of twenty is a child a decayed tooth. I know no form of infanticide worse than war: war is mass infanticide postponed to the age of twenty. And yet he accepts it, in the name of any number of other cults and does not apply his continuum thesis to it. Even as a scientist I cannot take his continuum seriously: if I did, I should have to go into mourning every time an egg dies unfertilized, every time two hundred million sperm fail to arrive and pierce the membrane. What's worse, I should have to go into mourning even when it does get fertilized, thinking of the one million nine hundred ninety-nine thousand nine hundred and ninety-nine sperm that die defeated by the single sperm that has pierced the membrane. They too are creatures of God. They too are alive and contain the elements that go to make up an individual. Has my colleague never observed them under a microscope? Has he never seen them swimming with their tails like a school of tadpoles? Has he never seen them toil and struggle against the pellucid zone, beating their heads desperately and knowing that to fail is to die? It's an agonizing spectacle. By ignoring it, my colleague is scarcely generous to his own sex. I have no wish to indulge in easy irony, but since he believes so much in life, how can he let billions and billions of sperm die without doing anything about it? Is this withholding of assistance or a crime? A crime, obviously: he too should be inside that cage. If he doesn't take his place there, and immediately, it means he has lied to us, that his sense of respectability is disturbed by those who say that the problem does not consist in letting the greatest number of individuals be born but in reducing as much as possible the misfortunes of those already in existence.

"Still, I'm prepared to overlook my colleague's insinuation of my complicity. At the most I can be accused of mistaken judgment, and not even a jury of life can hold me accountable for mistaken judgment. Besides it was nothing of the kind: it was simply a judgment and one for which I have no regrets. Pregnancy is not a punishment inflicted by nature to make you pay for the thrill of a moment. It's a miracle that ought to unfold with the same spontaneity that blesses the trees and fish. If it does not proceed in a normal way, you cannot ask a woman to lie flat on her back in a bed for months like a paralytic. In other words, you cannot ask her to give up her activity, her personality, her freedom. Do you demand it of a man, who enjoys that thrill much more? Obviously my colleague does not acknowledge for women the same right he acknowledges for men: the right to dispose of their own bodies. Obviously he considers the man a bee who is allowed to flit from flower to flower, the woman a genital system good only for procreation. It happens to many in our profession: the gynecologists' favorite patients are fat, placid brood mares with no problems of freedom. But we aren't here to judge the doctors. We're here to judge a woman accused of premeditated homicide, carried out by thought instead of by instruments. I reject the accusation on specific grounds. The day I diagnosed the pregnancy as normal, I saw how greatly relieved she was. The day I perceived that the fetus was dead, I saw how deeply she suffered. I said *fetus* and not *child*: science permits me to make this distinction. We all know that a fetus becomes a child only at the moment of viability, and that moment occurs in the ninth month; in exceptional cases, the seventh month. But let's even admit that it was no longer a fetus, that it was already a child: the crime would still not exist. My dear colleague, this woman did not desire the death of her child: she desired her own life. And unfortunately in certain cases our life is the death of another, the life of another is our death. We shoot at those who shoot at us. Written laws call it legitimate defense. If this woman unconsciously desired the death of her child, she did it in legitimate defense. Therefore, she is not guilty."

Then your father got up, and he was no longer crying. But as soon as he opened his mouth to speak, his chin began to tremble and the tears gushed forth again. Again he covered his eyes with his hands and fell back in his seat. "Then you don't care to speak?" the doctor said peevishly. Your father imperceptibly shook his head, as though answering no. "But you can't relinquish your vote," the other insisted. Your father redoubled his sobs. "Your vote, please!" Your father blew his nose without speaking. "Guilty or not?" Your father gave a long sigh and murmured: "Guilty." At that point something terrible happened: my friend turned and spat in his face. And, while he sat there pale and wiping his face, she shouted: "Coward! Hypocritical coward! You who phoned her just so she'd get rid of it. You who went into hiding for two months like a deserter. You who went to see her only because I begged you to. That's what you all do, isn't it? You get scared and leave us alone and, when you do come back to us, it's only in the name of paternity. For all that paternity costs you! A swaddled, ridiculous, fat stomach? Labor pains, the torture of nursing? The fruits of paternity are ladled out to you like a well-prepared soup or placed on the bed like an ironed shirt. You've nothing to do but give it a surname if you're married, not even that if you've succeeded in getting away. The woman has all the responsibility, all the suffering and insult. You call her a whore if she's made love to you. There's no male equivalent in the dictionary, and to invent one would be an error in semantics. For thousands of years you've been forcing your words on us, your precepts, your oppression. For thousands of years you've been making use of our bodies and giving us nothing back. For thousands of years you've imposed silence on us and consigned to us the job of being mothers. In every woman you look for a mother. You ask every woman to be a mother to you: even if she's your daughter. You say we don't have your muscles and then you exploit our labor even to get your shoes shined. You say we don't have your brains and then you exploit our intelligence even to administer the salary you bring home. Everlasting children, right up to old age you go on being children, needing to be fed, cleaned, served, advised, consoled, protected in your weaknesses and lazy habits. I despise you. And I despise myself for not being able to do without you, for not shouting at you more often: we're tired of being mothers to you. We're tired of this word, which you've sanctified in your own interest, your own selfishness. I ought to spit on you too, Doctor. All you see in a woman is a uterus and two ovaries, never a brain. You see a pregnant woman and think: 'First she has a good time and then she comes to me.' Haven't you ever had a good time, Doctor? Haven't you ever forgotten about the cult of life? You defend it so well at the cellular level that one might say you were envious of what your colleague calls the miracle of maternity. But no, I doubt it. That miracle would be a sacrifice for you. Being a man, you couldn't face it. We're not putting one woman on trial here, Doctor: we're putting all women on trial. And so I have the right to turn it around. Get one thing into your head, Doctor: maternity is not a moral duty. It's not even a biological fact. It's a conscious choice. This woman had made a conscious choice, and she didn't want to kill anyone. It's you who wanted to kill her, Doctor, by denying her even the use of her own intellect. That's why you should be the one in the cage, and not for withholding assistance from billions of stupid spermatozoa but for attempted femicide. In view of all this, it goes without saying that the accused is not guilty."

Then my boss got up with an expression of false embarrassment. He said he didn't know how to pronounce an opinion, since he felt like an outsider on this jury. The others were linked to the defendant by professional or emotional ties that included the child; he, on the other hand, was merely her employer. As such, he could only rejoice in the fact that things had turned out the way they had: even with every wish to be magnanimous, he had always considered that pregnancy an obstacle. Or worse, a catastrophe that would cost him a good deal of money. Just think of the salary she would have to be paid, according to an absurd and objectionable law, even in her months of inactivity. The child had been wise, wiser than the mother. Moreover, by dying, it had protected the name of the firm. What would the public have thought on seeing one of his employees, unmarried to boot, with a newborn baby in her arms? He wasn't ashamed to admit it: had the woman accepted his offer, he would have helped her to get rid of the untimely infant. But he wasn't only a businessman, he was a man. And the jurors who had preceded him, the two male jurors, of course, had aroused second thoughts in his mind. The doctor through logic and morality, the child's father through grief. On reflection, he could not help aligning himself with the reasoning of the former and the sorrow of the latter. A child belongs in equal measure to the father and the mother: if a crime had been committed, it was a question of a double crime, since, in addition to eliminating the life of an infant, it had shattered the life of an adult man. Of course, it was necessary to decide whether the crime had been committed or not: but were there any doubts on that score? Was any more crushing proof needed than the testimony offered by the doctor? The doctor had been too indulgent in speaking of a general selfishness. He, the woman's employer, could disclose the specific motive and reason. The defendant had been afraid that the famous trip would be assigned to a rival colleague. That was why she had jumped out of bed and departed, with no concern for the life she carried in her womb. With no compassion. Let her ally go ahead and spit, let her go ahead and insult him. He found the defendant guilty.

Then my eyes sought out my father and mother. And in silence I implored them, for they were my last hope for salvation. They answered me with a disheartened look. They seemed exhausted, much older than when the trial had begun. Their heads hung forward as though their necks couldn't support the weight, their bodies trembled as though they were cold, and everything in them gave way to a sadness that set them apart from the others, uniting them in a single despair. They held each other's hands for support. Hand in hand, they asked permission to remain seated. Permission was granted, and then I saw them confer: to decide, I suppose, who would speak first. It was he who spoke first. He said: "I have had two sorrows. The first sorrow was in knowing that the child existed, and the second in knowing it didn't exist any more. I hope I'll be spared a third sorrow: seeing my daughter convicted. I don't know how these things happened. None of you can know since none can enter into the souls of others. But this is my daughter, and to a father his children are not guilty. Never." Then my mother spoke. She said: "She's my little girl. She'll always be my little girl. And my little girl can't do anything bad. When she wrote me that she was expecting a child, I wrote back: 'If you've decided on it, that means it's right.' If she had written me that she didn't want it, I would have answered the same thing. It's not for us to judge, nor for you. You have no right to accuse or defend her, because you're not inside her mind and heart. None of your testimony is worth anything. There's only one witness here who could explain what happened. And this witness is the child who cannot . . ." Then the others interrupted her, in chorus: "The child, the child!" And I seized the bars of the cage, shouting: "Not the child! Not the child!" And it was while I was shouting like this that . . .

* * *

YES, IT WAS WHILE I WAS SHOUTING LIKE THIS that I heard your voice: "Mother!" And I felt a sense of loss—of emptiness—because it was the first time anyone had called me Mother, and because it was the first time I was hearing your voice, and it wasn't the voice of a child. It was the voice of an adult, of a man. And I thought: "He was a man!" Then I thought: "He was a man, he'll condemn me." Finally I thought: "I want to see him!" And my eyes searched everywhere, in the cage, outside the cage, among the benches, beyond the benches, on the floor, on the walls. But they didn't find you. You weren't there. There was only the quiet of a tomb. And in this quiet of a tomb your voice was heard again: "Mother! Let me speak, Mother. Don't be afraid. There's no need to be afraid of the truth. Besides, it's already been said. Each of them has spoken a truth, and you know it: it was you who taught me that truth is made up of many different truths. Those who have accused you are right and so are those who have defended you, those who have absolved you and those who have condemned you. But those judgments don't count. Your father and mother are right in saying one can't enter into the souls of others and that the only witness is myself. Only I, Mother, can say that you killed me without killing me. Only I can explain how you did it and why. I hadn't asked to be born, Mother. No one asks for it. In nothingness there is no will. There is no choice. There's nothingness, that's all. When we're wrenched away and we realize we've started out, we don't even wonder who wanted it and whether it's good or bad. We simply accept and then wait to see if we like it. I found very early that I liked it. Even through your fear, your hesitation, you were so good in convincing me that to be born is beautiful and to escape from nothingness a joy. Once you're born, you mustn't get discouraged, you said: not even at suffering, not even at dying. If one dies, it means one was born, that one emerged from nothingness, and nothing is worse than nothingness: the worst is having to say that one has not existed. Your faith seduced me, your arrogance. It really seemed like the arrogance of those remote times when life had exploded in the way you told me. I believed you, Mother. Along with the water in which I was immersed, I drank in your every thought. And your every thought had the flavor of a revelation. Could it have happened otherwise? My body was only a plan that developed in you, by virtue of you; my mind was only a promise that was realized in you, by virtue of you. All I learned was what you gave me; what you didn't give me I couldn't know; my drafts of light and awareness were you. If you were challenging everything so as to lead me into life, I thought life must truly be a sublime gift.

"But then your uncertainties and doubts increased, and you started wavering between flattery and threats, tenderness and resentment, courage and fear. To wash away your fear one day you bestowed on me the decision to exist, Mother. You claimed you had obeyed an order of mine, not your own choice. You actually accused me of being your master: you my victim, not I yours. And you went on to reproach me, blaming me for making you suffer. You even reached the point of challenging me by explaining what life was like: a trap devoid of freedom, of happiness, of love. A well of slavery and violence that I wouldn't be able to get out of. You never tired of showing me that there's no salvation in the ant heap, that no one can escape its sinister laws. Magnolia trees are there for women to be flung down on, chocolate to be eaten by those who don't need it; tomorrow is first a man shot for a piece of bread and then it's a bag of dirty underpants. Your sad fairy tales always ended with a question: Was it really time for me to emerge from my peaceful nest and come forth? You never told me that one can pick magnolia blossoms without dying, that one can eat chocolate without humiliation, that tomorrow can be better than yesterday. And when you realized it, it was too late: I was already committing suicide. Don't cry, Mother: I realize you did it for love, to prepare me for the day when I would first be struck by the horror of existence. It's not true, Mother, that you don't believe in love. You believe in it so much that you torture yourself because you see so little of it, and because what little you see is never perfect. You're made of love. But is it enough to believe in love if you don't believe in life? No sooner did I see that you didn't believe in life, that you were making such an effort to live there and bring me to live there, than I allowed myself my first and last choice: that of refusing to be born, denying you the moon for the second time. By then I could do so, Mother. My mind was no longer your mind: I had one of my own. A small one, perhaps, only the outline of one, but still able to draw this conclusion: if life is a torment, what's the use of it? You had never told me why one is born. And you had been honest enough not to deceive me with the legends you who are born have invented to console yourselves: the omnipotent God who creates in his image and likeness, the search for good, the race to paradise. Your only explanation was that you too had been born, and before you your mother, before your mother, your mother's mother: all the way back into a yesterday whose traces were lost. In short, one was born because others had been born so that others would be born: in a proliferation similar to oneself. If it weren't to happen this way, you told me one evening, the human species would be wiped out. Or rather it wouldn't exist. But why should it exist, why must it exist, Mother? What's the purpose? I'll tell you, Mother: an expectation of death, of nothingness. In my universe, which you called the egg, the purpose existed: it was to be born. But in your world the purpose is only to die: life is a death sentence. I don't see why I should have had to emerge from nothingness just to return to nothingness."

Then I understood how deep and irreparable was the evil I had inflicted on you and on myself, on the things in which I force myself to believe: to be born to be happy, free, good, to fight in the name of happiness, of freedom, of goodness, to be born to venture, to know, to discover, to invent—so as not to die. In the grip of panic, I kept hoping this was all a dream, a nightmare from which I'd emerge to find you alive, a child inside me, and begin all over, without getting frightened, without showing impatience, without renouncing the faith called hope. I shook the cage, telling myself it didn't exist. The cage resisted. It was really a cage and really a court, a trial had really been held and you had judged me guilty because I judged myself guilty. You had convicted me because I convicted myself. All that remained was to decide the penalty, and this was obvious: to reject life and return to nothingness with you. I held out my arms to you. I begged you to take me away with you at once. And you came close to me, and said: "But I forgive you, Mother. Don't cry. I'll be born some other time."

Splendid words, Child, but only words. All the sperm and all the ova on earth united in all possible combinations could never create a new you, what you were and what you might have been. You'll never be reborn. You'll never come back. And I go on talking to you out of pure desperation.

* * *

FOR DAYS YOU'VE BEEN LOCKED INSIDE THERE, lifeless but without departing. The woman doctor is puzzled and frightened. I might die, she says, if you're not removed. I understand completely and, what's more, I have no intention of punishing myself to that extent, using you to apply the self-condemnation of that absurd trial. The harshness of my regret is enough for me. At the same time, however, I'm in no hurry to remove you and it would be difficult to single out the reason. Is it perhaps the habit of our being together, falling asleep together, waking up together, while knowing myself to be alone without being alone? Perhaps the illogical suspicion that it's all a mistake and that it would be a good idea to wait? Or perhaps because to go back to being what I was before you doesn't interest me any more? I had so yearned to become once again the master of my fate. Now that I am, I don't care. Here's one more reality that you lost the chance to discover: you wear yourself out in the pursuit of wealth or love or freedom, you do everything to gain some right, and once it's gained, you take no pleasure in it. Either you waste it or ignore it, often thinking how you'd like to go back, start the battle and torment all over again. To have realized your dream makes you feel lost. Blessed is he who can say: "I want to go forward, I don't want to arrive." Cursed is he who insists: "I want to get there." To arrive is to die, all you can allow yourself are some stops along the way. If you could at least persuade me that you've been only a stop, that one death doesn't stop life, that life had no need of you, that this pain served some purpose for something or somebody. But whose purpose is served by a child who dies and a mother who relinquishes being a mother? Moralists, jurists, theologians, reformers? In that case, one might ask who will make the most of this story and what will be the verdict of their court. Do I deserve people's solidarity or their insults? Have I performed a service for moralists or jurists, theologians or reformers? Have I sinned by driving you to suicide and killing you? Or have I sinned by attributing to you a soul that you didn't possess? Just listen to them discussing it, hear how they shout: she's offended God, no, she's offended women; she's belittled a problem, no, she's made a contribution to it; she's understood that life is sacred, no, she's made it a joke. Almost as though the dilemma. to be or not to be, could be resolved by one court sentence or another, one law or another, as though it weren't up to every creature to resolve it by and for himself. Almost as though to divine one truth did not open up the possibility of an opposite truth, and that both weren't valid. What's the purpose of all their trials and litigation? To find out what's permissible and what isn't? To decide wherein lies justice? You were right, Child: it lies in all of them. There are also many kinds of awareness: I am that doctor and his woman colleague, my friend and the boss, my mother and father, your father and you. I am what each of you said I was. And before me stretch valleys of sadness where pride blooms in vain.

* * *

YOUR FATHER HAS WRITTEN ME AGAIN. This time it's a letter that makes me think. He says: "I know you well enough not to try to console you by saying that you did well to sacrifice the child for yourself rather than yourself for the child. You know better than I do (it was you who shouted it when you threw me out) that a woman is not a hen, that not all hens hatch their eggs, that some abandon them and others drink them. Nor do we condemn them for this, or no more than we condemn nature for killing by earthquakes and disease. I also know you well enough not to remind you that the cruelty of nature and hens contains an element of logic and wisdom: if every possibility for existence became actual existence, we would die for lack of space. You know better than I that no one is indispensable, that the world would have kept going just the same if Homer and Icarus and Leonardo da Vinci and Jesus Christ had not been born: the child you wanted to lose leaves behind no empty space, his disappearance does no harm either to society or to the future. It wounds only you, and beyond all measure, because your mind has magnified a tragedy that may not even be a tragedy at all. (My poor darling, you've discovered that to think means to suffer, that to be intelligent means to be unhappy. Too bad a third fundamental point has escaped you: pain is the salt of life and without it we would not be human.) So I don't write to console you. I write to congratulate you, to acknowledge that you've won. But not because you've shaken off the slavery of a pregnancy and maternity, but because you've succeeded in not yielding to the need for others, including the need for God. Just the opposite has happened to me. Oh, yes. Envy of those who believe in God so assailed me these last months that it became a temptation, and I yielded to that temptation. I recognize it when I see how tired I am. God is an exclamation point by which all the broken fragments are glued back together: if one believes, it means he's tired and no longer able to get along by himself. You're not tired for you're the apotheosis of doubt. God for you is a question mark, or rather the first question mark in an infinite series of question marks. And only those who torture themselves with questions can go forward; only those who don't give in to the comfort of believing in God can begin again: contradict themselves again, be unworthy of themselves again, give themselves over once more to sorrow. Our friend tells me the child is still inside you and you refuse to do anything about it, almost as though you were making use of it to punish yourself for inconsistency and forbid yourself to live. I suppose she's told me so that I might urge you not to persist in this folly. Rather than urging you, I'm just telling you that you won't persist for long. You love life too much to be deaf to its call. When the call comes, you'll obey it like that dog of Jack London's who goes howling after the wolves to become a wolf among them."

Tomorrow indeed we're going home. And though to me the word *tomorrow* seems like an affront to you, a threat to me, I can't help looking around and realizing that tomorrow is a day brimming with opportunity.

* * *

THEY GREETED ME WITH GREAT ENTHUSIASM, as though I'd been sick with a foot or ear ailment and was now beginning to convalesce. They congratulated me for carrying my work through to the end despite-the-difficulties. They took me out to eat. And never a word about you. When I tried to say something, they assumed an expression between evasiveness and embarrassment: almost as though I were bringing up a disagreeable subject and they wanted to say let's-not-think-about-it-any-more-what-has-been-has-been. Later my friend took me aside and, as though to remind me of an important appointment, told me she had consulted the doctor, who had said that I mustn't count on your spontaneous departure: if I don't get you removed, I'll die of septicemia. I must decide; it would be paradoxical if, to right the scales, you were to kill me. I still have so many things to do. You never started any, but I did. I have to go on with my career and prove I'm as good as a man. I have to fight against the comfort of those exclamation points, I have to get people to ask themselves the whys more often. I have to stamp out my self-pity and convince myself that pain is not the salt of life. The salt of life is happiness, and happiness exists: it consists in the pursuit of it. Finally I still have to clarify that mystery they call love. Not the kind that's consummated in a bed by touching each other. I mean the kind I was about to know with you. I miss you, Child. I miss you as I'd miss an arm, an eye, my voice, and yet I miss you less than yesterday, less than this morning. It's strange. One could say that hour by hour the torment fades, to be placed between parentheses. The wolves have already begun to call me and it doesn't matter if they're still far away: as soon as they get close, I know I'll follow them. Have I really suffered so deeply and so long? I ask myself in disbelief. I once read in a book that we're aware of the harshness of the suffering we've endured only when it's over, and then we exclaim in astonishment: how was I able to bear such hell? It must really be like that, and life is extraordinary. Our wounds heal with astonishing speed. If we didn't bear the scars, we wouldn't even remember that blood had flowed. And eventually even the scars disappear. They fade away and finally vanish. That will happen to me too. Or will it? I must make it happen, because I have to, I need to. I'm taking down your portrait from the wall now; I'm going to stop frightening myself with your wide-open eyes. And I'm tearing up the other photographs. And this cradle that I kept like a coffin, I'm breaking it to pieces and throwing it in the incinerator. And putting away your wardrobe to give to someone else, or perhaps I'll rip it to shreds. I'll make the appointment with the doctor, I'll tell him I agree, one of these days you'll have to be removed. And I might even call your father or somebody, and go to bed with him tonight: I've had enough of chastity. You're dead but I'm alive. So alive that I don't regret it, and I don't accept trials, I don't accept verdicts, not even your forgiveness. The wolves are here, close by, and I have the strength to give birth to you another hundred times without imploring God or anyone else for help . . .

God, what pain! I feel ill, all of a sudden. What is it? The knifelike stabs again. They go all the way to my brain to pierce it as they did before. I'm sweating. I feel feverish. Our moment has come, Child: the moment to separate us. And I don't want to. I don't want them to tear you away with a spoon, to throw you in the garbage with the dirty cotton and gauze. I wouldn't want that. But I have no choice. If I don't rush to the hospital and have them tear you out of my insides where you go on clinging, you'll kill me. And this I can't allow. I mustn't. You were wrong to say that I don't believe in life, Child. I do believe in it. I like it, even with all its infamies, and I mean to live it at all cost. I'm running, Child. And I bid you a firm good-bye.

* * *

THERE'S A WHITE CEILING above me, and alongside me you rest in a glass. They didn't want me to see you, but I persuaded them by saying it was my right, and they put you there, with a frown of disapproval. I look at you, finally. And I feel cheated because you have really nothing in common with the child in the photograph. You're not a child: you're an egg. A gray egg floating in pink alcohol, inside which one can see nothing. You ended long before they realized it: you never arrived at having nails and skin and the infinite riches I attributed to you.

Creature of my imagination, you barely succeeded in realizing the wish for two hands and two feet, something that resembled a body, the outline of a face with a little nose and two microscopic eyes. It was a little fish I loved, after all. And for the love of a little fish, I invented a calvary which has cost me the risk of dying myself. I won't accept it. Why didn't I get you removed before? Why did I waste so much time letting you poison me? I'm ill, they all look alarmed. They've put needles in my right arm and left wrist; from the needles slender tubes extend and rise like serpents up to the feeding bottles. The nurse stands by with wads of cotton. Every so often the doctor comes in with another doctor and they exchange remarks that I can't make out but that sound like threats. I'd give a lot to see my friend or your father arrive, better still my parents. It seemed to me I heard their voices. Instead no one comes except those two in their white jackets: is one of them the doctor who condemned me? A moment ago he got angry. He said: "Double the dose!" The dose of what? Of pain, of sorrow? I'd gone through it already, must I start again? Then he said: "Hurry up, don't you see that it's going?" What's going? A needle, a person, my life? Life can't go away if you don't want it to: no one dies here. Not even you; you were already dead. Dead without knowing what it means to be alive: without knowing colors, tastes, odors, sounds, feelings, thought. I'm sorry: for you and for me. I feel humiliated, because what good is it to fly like a seagull if you don't produce other seagulls that will produce others and still others who may fly? What good is it to play like children if you don't produce other children who will produce others and still others who will play and enjoy themselves? You should have fought and won. You gave in too soon, resigned yourself too quickly: you weren't made for life. How can anyone get scared by a couple of fairy tales, over two or three warnings? You were like your father: he finds it comfortable to rest in God, you found it comfortable to rest by not being born. Which one of us has betrayed life? Not I. I'm very tired, I have no sensation in my legs, at intervals my eyes cloud over and silence envelops me like a buzzing of wasps. And yet, look, I don't give in. Look, I hold on. We're so different. I mustn't fall asleep. I must stay awake and think. If I think, maybe I'll hold out. How long have you been in that glass? For hours, days, years? Days perhaps and to me it seems years: I can't go on leaving you in a glass. I must find a more dignified place for you: but where? Perhaps at the foot of the magnolia. But the magnolia is far away: it belongs to the time when I too was a child. The present has no magnolias. Not even my home. I should take you home. In the morning, however. Now it's night; the white ceiling is turning black. And it's cold. Better put on your overcoat to go out. Come on, let's go: I'll carry you. I'd like to hold you in my arms, Child. But you're so tiny: I can't hold you in my arms. I can rest you on the palm of one hand, that's all. So long as a puff of wind doesn't blow you away. Now there's something I don't understand: a puff of wind can blow you away, and still you weigh so much I'm staggering. Give me your hand, please: like this. Good. Look, now it's you who's leading me, guiding me. But then you're not an egg, you're not a little fish: you're a child! You already come up to my knee. No, to my heart. No, to my shoulder. No, above my shoulder. You're not a child, you're a man! A man with strong and gentle fingers. I need them now, I'm an old woman. I can't even go down the steps if you don't hold me up. Do you remember when we went up and down these stairs, careful not to fall, each clinging to the other in an embrace of complicity? Remember when I taught you to go by yourself, you'd been walking for only a little time, and laughing we counted the stairs? Remember how you learned by holding on to everything, panting, while I followed you with outstretched hands? And the day when we quarreled because you wouldn't listen to my advice? Later I was sorry. I wanted to beg your forgiveness but I couldn't. I sought out your eyes and meanwhile you were seeking mine, until suddenly a smile appeared on your lips and I understood that you had understood. Then what happened? My mind is clouding, my eyelids are like lead. Is it sleep or the end? I mustn't give in to sleep, to the end. Help me to stay awake, answer me: was it hard to use your wings? Did they all shoot at you? Did you shoot back in your turn? Did they oppress you in the ant heap? Did you give in to disappointment and rage or did you stand upright like a strong tree? Did you discover if happiness, freedom, goodness, love exist? I hope my advice was some help to you. I hope you never howled that dreadful blasphemy "why was I born?" I hope you decided it was worth the trouble: at the cost of suffering, at the cost of dying. I'm so proud of having drawn you forth out of nothingness at the cost of suffering, at the cost of dying. It's awfully cold and the white ceiling is black. But here we are, here's the magnolia. Pick a flower. I never succeeded in doing it, but you will. Stand on tiptoe, reach out your arm. Like this. Where are you? You were here, you were holding me up, you were tall, you were a man. And now you're no more. There's only a jar of alcohol where something is floating that didn't want to become a man or woman, that I didn't help to become a man or woman. Why should I have, you ask me, why should you have? Why, because life exists, Child! The cold goes away when I say that life exists, my drowsiness goes away, I feel I'm life itself. A light is on. I hear voices. Someone is running, crying out in despair. But elsewhere a thousand, a hundred thousand children are being born, and mothers of future children: life doesn't need you or me. You're dead. Maybe I'm dying too. But it doesn't matter. Because life doesn't die.

ORIANA FALLACI is international correspondent for the distinguished Milan journal *L'Europeo.* Her articles and interviews appear frequently in the *New York Sunday Times Magazine*, the *New York Review of Books*, the *New York Post*, the *Washington Post*, *MS.* and the *New Republic.* She has received many awards including the Italian equivalent of the Pulitzer Prize, awarded to her twice, and a special citation from the Overseas Press Club.

Ms. Fallaci is the author of *The Useless Sex*, *Penelope at War*, *The Egotists*, *If the Sun Dies*, *Nothing and So Be It*, the result of her experiences in Vietnam, and, most recently, *Interviews with History.*

FREEPORT MEMORIAL LIBRARY
3 1489 00089 2107

DISCARDED BY
FREEPORT
MEMORIAL LIBRARY

FREEPORT MEMORIAL LIBRARY